APOCALYPSE WINTER

APOCALYPSE WINTER

Tyler H. Jolley
David J. West

I dedicate this to Dinty Moore beef stew.
The heartiest canned stew on the market to this day.

CHAPTER 1

Matt opened his eyes. The frosted glass of his cryopod obscured the people standing over him, watching him, shadowlike. Were they his parents? Scientists who worked at the cryovault? He panted, struggling to get enough air. Panic washed over him like a cold river. He banged on the glass, screaming, "Let me out! Let me out!"

The shadows remained, observing as if he were no more than a bug to be examined under a microscope. They did nothing to help his feeble attempts to escape his cryocoffin.

"Help! Help me!"

He gasped and sat up, his rumpled blankets tangled about him on the floor of a research and development building they had nicknamed the Sev.

We're still here.

The night before was numbing to say the least. They had lost three friends and drowned their sorrows and injuries with old beer and a dance party. The reality of today weighed down on Matt.

"Morning," came a voice.

Matt rubbed the sleep from his eyes.

Darin lay wide awake in a huddle of blankets, Stacy sprawled across him. "Rough night?" Darin asked.

"Bad dream. You?" Matt responded.

"Probably the best night I think I've ever had, actually," Darin said.

Stacy, still asleep, snuggled closer with a smile on her face, despite her injuries.

"Maybe we should go and get the supplies, first-aid kits, clothes, and things—and let them sleep it off?" Matt stood and weaved his way past a sleeping Catherine, Stacy, and Justin. The party from the night before had lingered into the early morning. He wandered over to get a drink of water from one of the barrels to try to shake the sleep out of him. "If we run, it shouldn't take the two of us too long."

Darin nodded as he pulled himself out from under Stacy. She murmured, her arm reaching for him like he was her pillow, but she remained asleep. "Wasn't sure I could move out from under her."

Matt nodded and offered a refilled canteen to Darin.

"Thanks." He took a good, long swallow. "I always wanted to party with the teenagers when I was a kid."

Matt looked at him with a raised eyebrow, trying to decide if he was joking or not. It *was* strange though, Darin was put into cryosleep at twelve—five years younger than Matt, but during his time out with Westbrook he'd aged to twenty years old. Making him Matt's senior.

"I really did," Darin reaffirmed.

Matt still wasn't sure if he was serious. "I figure if we

hurry, we can get back with any salvageable gear and the first-aid kits before they're even all awake." He glanced around at the mess and the slumbering bodies strewn about the floor. "We did party pretty hard, didn't we?"

"Any harder and Spuds Mackenzie would have shown up."

Matt chuckled, remembering the party dog, and moved a bit of debris from the previous night's party from in front of the door.

Darin took the handkerchief from the doorknob hole, and when no smoke poured in through the broken handle, he opened the door. He squinted at the brightness of the morning, filtered through gray clouds. "You wouldn't even know a volcano went off last night. Where's the smoke?"

Matt stepped out and let the hazy light cascade across his face. "I don't know. I'm just glad it's gone. I wasn't sure I would ever see a day like this again."

Darin grinned. "When you see every kind of weather there is, there must be a good day once in a while."

"My dad used to say, 'A broken clock is right twice a day.'"

"He's right."

"Hey! Where are you guys going?" Catherine asked. "Don't go out there. It isn't safe."

Matt turned to the sleepy-eyed girl. "Take a look for yourself."

She met them outside, a blanket wrapped around her burned shoulder, and joined in their amazement at the calmness of the forest outside the Sev. "I can almost see the sun through the clouds." She pointed up, and Matt laughed. "What's so funny?"

"You pointed at the wrong spot. It's morning. The sun is over there."

"How do you know? That's not east," Darin countered.

Matt shook his head. "It's where I've noticed the most light every morning."

"Does your compass even work?" Darin argued.

"No."

"Then you don't know which way is east. Besides, I think the sun is over there." Darin pointed in an altogether new direction.

Catherine squinted as she looked up at the gray sky. "I think I can see *three* suns behind the clouds."

"Three suns is crazy. We aren't on Tatooine," Matt said with a laugh.

"Aren't we on a crazy alien landscape, though?" Catherine taunted. "I wouldn't be surprised if sand people tried to ambush us next."

Darin scowled. "Don't even joke about that. Last thing I want to do with this crazy weather is fight a zombie horde of freaks."

Catherine winced. "Sorry. I'd be happy to see almost any other people."

"Not if they were trying to kill you," Darin said.

Cody ambled up to the group. "What're you guys doin' up, anyway?"

"We're going to go get the first-aid kits and look for some food and clothes at the camp while the going is good. We'll be right back." Matt turned to Catherine. "You can stay here . . . if you want."

"You can keep an eye on things, especially Stacy, please," Darin added.

"All right, I will. You two be careful, though. This weather is bound to change any minute, you know."

"I'm going with them. And we'll be careful," Cody said.

They walked back along the path they had come on to get to the Sev, and Matt marveled silently at how yesterday, freak storms had destroyed everything and taken three of his friends' lives. How did Camp New Beginnings suddenly resurrect itself? It was like they were being played with by some terrible gamemaster. He turned to Darin. "Did you ever see a movie called *The Dungeon Master,* where the main guy was being transported into all kinds of worlds by this evil DM, and it kept changing? This reminds me of that in a way."

"No, I never saw it. Snuck into *Goonies* once."

"Well, this was a little different. Scarier, I guess, like *Nightmare on Elm Street.*"

Darin shook his head. "You all talk about all these pop culture references like it was yesterday, and for you guys, it was yesterday, but I was twelve. I didn't pay attention to a lot of that like you teenagers. I rode my bike and went swimming, but it was all over once I was with crazy old Westbrook. I didn't get to enjoy any of that stuff. It was all just work, work, work. Do this, do that. I didn't get a life like you guys."

Cody shook his head. "Sorry."

"It's all right now. I just feel out of place and alone."

He glanced back toward the hill concealing the Sev from their view and said softly, "It's nice to be wanted."

"Stacy?" Matt asked.

Darin looked at him and muttered, "Yeah," before taking a few quicker steps, signaling an end to the conversation.

Camp New Beginnings had transformed into something out of *Mad Max*. Hardened black lava covered the back part of camp. A black brick road to destruction. The cabins had been burned, leaving piles of pullies and cables intertwined with scorched wood and hot coals. The trio rummaged through the buildings that had survived the apocalyptic crescendo and found a couple of first-aid kits, complete with salve for burns and extra bandages.

Darin found a couple of forgotten MREs. "You never know when these might come in handy."

Matt nodded. "Good call. Let's hurry back to the others."

They jogged along, keeping a good pace, then Matt paused. "Hey, wait up a sec."

Darin stopped. "What is it?"

"Something looks weird over there. Something is moving the grass, but there's no wind."

"An animal?" Cody asked.

"I haven't seen any animals this whole time," Matt said.

"Me neither, but if it's a rabbit or a chicken, it's going down." Cody crouched into a hunter's stance.

"Let's be careful," Matt urged.

"Right, we don't want to scare it away," Darin said.

"I don't think it's an animal. The grass is movin' too

weird. Plus, it's where me and Nathan buried your belt," Cody said.

Darin stopped his crouching approach. "Then let's go back to the others. We've got people to take care of. Who cares about where the belt bomb went off?"

"I want to check it out." Matt crouched next to Cody and crept toward the swaying grass. "With all the natural disasters, we should make sure it's safe. I don't want to lose anyone else."

Cody nodded. "That's true."

"Plus," Matt said, "that's the way we have to go to get to the mountain, so we're going to pass it anyway. It won't hurt to make sure the ground's stable for us before we bring everyone over here."

Cody followed him.

At the edge of the billowing grass, Matt stopped dead in his tracks.

Darin caught up to them and looked down. "Whoa!"

Matt whistled. "That is one big sinkhole."

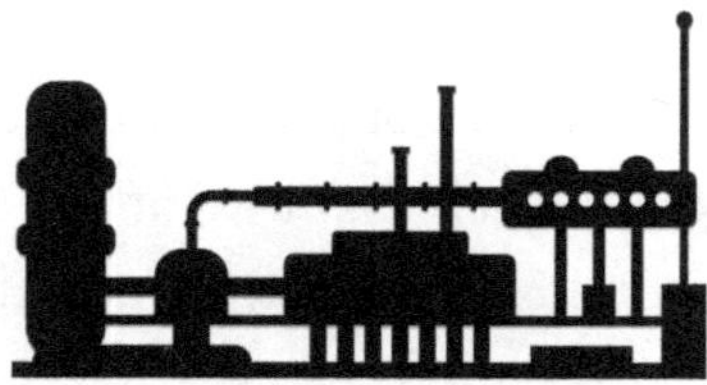

CHAPTER 2

Matt, Cody, and Darin stood around the forbidding black hole as if it were a gravesite. The ten-foot by ten-foot chasm—about the size of an elevator shaft—had no bottom in sight.

Cody whistled and looked at Darin. "Just think, you were wearing that thing."

"How did a weight-belt bomb make a hole that deep?" Matt asked.

Darin shook his head. "It didn't. Cody must have placed it right on top of a small volcanic fissure."

"But it's so big," Matt exclaimed. He kicked a small stone into the dark unknown.

It clanged far below, an oddly familiar sound of rock hitting metal.

"Maybe it's just a tunnel," Cody said. "A tunnel that goes to the Sev."

"Under the ground? So you think it's connected?" Matt asked. "We didn't see any tunnels running this far over when we explored the Sev, though."

"Maybe not to the Sev, then," Cody said. "But could it be connected to the cryovault?"

"I think that's gotta be too far away." Matt shook his head and pointed to the mountain. "I just know we need to get to the mountain and find my parents."

Cody put a hand on Matt's shoulder and smiled. "But . . . you want to investigate first."

Within the short few days they'd been together, Cody had unlocked Matt. His humor. His curiosity and ideas.

Matt nodded. "This all makes sense!" He continued to nod. "I didn't put two and two together until now. There must be a tunnel system or something. Cody, you're right. Back at the Sev, there was a blueprint with tunnels on it, but I didn't realize what it was. Maybe we can get to the mountain this way. Underground."

"I don't know about that," Darin said.

"Look," Matt said, "let me just take a look first. If it's not a tunnel, then we'll forget about it, but if it is, then wouldn't you think we would be safer underground?"

Darin shrugged.

"We've had so many people die up here that a tunnel might be safer. The natural disasters wouldn't touch us."

Darin examined the base of the hole. "Seems like a death trap to me. Even if you reached the bottom safely, you might end up just crawling around, not knowing where you are." He kicked at a cooled bit of lava rock that had reached the edge and dripped into the hole.

"It's worth a look," Matt persisted.

"Can you see the bottom? I sure can't." Cody peered down the hole.

They stood a moment longer. The breeze blowing

up from the shaft stopped, and the grasses alongside the open abyss went still again. Matt looked at Darin and Cody and then up at the sky, wondering if some terrible new weather disaster was about to be sprung upon them. But the sound of gears grinding didn't come. For now, they were safe.

A moment passed, and Cody said, "Well, we better be getting back to the others and fixing up everyone's burns." He and Darin headed back the way they'd come.

We all agreed that we would go to the mountain. Everyone is injured. This could be a better and safer way, Matt thought.

He took a step after them but stopped. "Wait, we can't give up on this opportunity. I think it's still worth checking out."

"How?" Darin argued with gruffness. He held his fist up and whistled as he slammed it into the palm of his other hand, simulating Matt falling down the long shaft. "Splat."

"If I can find a safe way to get down there, can we check it out?" Matt propositioned. It felt like he was asking an older brother to take him to the movies or something.

Darin nodded with a chuckle. "Okay, I give. If you can find a safe way in there, I'll help you. But there isn't a safe way in. Done deal."

"Do you promise that *if* there is a way, though?" Matt asked. He didn't have an older brother, but he still felt like he had to negotiate with Darin and get his permission.

"I promise." Darin put his hands up in surrender.

"Good, 'cause I saw some rope back at one of those cabins before the snowstorm hit. I'll go find it, and we can go down and check out my theory."

Darin frowned as he peered into the abyss. "Better be a helluva long rope."

"I'll hurry. I know right where I saw it." Matt ignored his warning—even though his Scouts training told him Darin was right about the length of rope.

"I'll help," Cody said.

Matt and Cody raced across to where one of the cabins had been knocked down but now stood up again. He didn't want to think about how that had happened. It was too . . . crazy. Maybe the avalanche had only made it look like they had fallen over, and it had been an illusion because of the cold. But then, the lodge had fallen over and killed Nathan and was back up again. No, something didn't add up about old Camp New Beginnings. He shook the thought out of his mind. It was an apocalypse, after all. Nothing seemed right during an apocalypse.

Matt found the rope lying coiled in a heap beside a ramshackle shed. "Found it!"

Cody slapped his thigh. "Giddy-up."

Matt snapped the dirty old rope taut to check its strength. Dust and rope fibers floated up in front of his face. He shrugged. "Seems good to me."

"Let me help ya," Cody said as he picked up the dragging portion.

They rushed back to where they had left Darin beside the hole.

"We found a rope," Matt said.

"Good for us," Darin said. "One step closer to dying."

Matt and Cody piled the rope next to the hole.
"Let's go!" Darin chided. "Let's get the others."
"We're coming," Cody said.

CHAPTER 3

"Where have you guys been?" Stacy asked as Matt and Darin came through the door.

"Didn't Catherine tell you?" Matt asked.

"She did, but I want to hear it from you guys. Is the weather getting crazy again out there?" she asked, brightening as Darin produced a first-aid kit and sat down next to her.

"No, it's actually pretty nice, you know, for the apocalypse," Matt said.

"Yo, chief, what'd you find for us?" Justin asked, wiping the sleep from his eyes.

Matt tossed him a first-aid kit. "Something to take care of everyone's burns a little better. Let's get everyone patched up, and then I've got something cool to show you guys."

"Somethin' cool." Cody nodded.

"It isn't cool. It's a hole." Darin rolled his eyes.

"A hole?" Justin asked.

"A hole?" Stacy repeated.

"A hole," Catherine said.

Darin, Justin, and Cody laughed.

"A-hole finds a hole," Justin said with a laugh.

Matt shook his head, trying to regain his composure. Why couldn't they see the importance of his discovery? "Look, guys, we should check this out. Darin has already promised he would help."

"Lance-Darin?" Stacy questioned, as if she were a disapproving mother.

"He wants to slide down a rope and look around. We'll all just help pull him back up." Darin smiled. "Now, let's take a look at your foot."

"Sounds dangerous," Catherine said.

Matt huffed and raised his voice a little. "It's worth it, and it'll just be me going in."

"We can't afford to lose anyone." She frowned.

"I think it's worth the risk," Cody said. "Could be a shortcut or something."

Darin broke in, "If the rope is long enough, he'll be fine. We can just pull him back up."

"Let me help you," Catherine said as Darin began undoing the old bandage on Stacy's foot.

Stacy gritted her teeth and squeezed Darin's hand until his knuckles turned white. Catherine gingerly applied salve and eased Stacy's foot into an extra-large sock and new shoe. Darin covered the shoe with a thick garbage bag and duct-taped it around her pants leg at her calf to keep it dry.

"We'll have to check your foot again tonight, put more salve on it, and change the sock." Catherine smiled at Stacy.

Matt applied ointment to Justin's burns that he couldn't reach himself. They looked worse than they had last night, but he held his cool better than Stacy had, only flinching a little at the salve application.

"It tickles," he said as Matt paused in applying the cream.

"Dude, I don't ever want to tickle another dude," Matt said. "Don't tell me that."

"Can I smear some of that on my shoulder?" Catherine reached for the jar.

Matt handed it to her. "Let me help you."

She slowly smiled, then nodded. She held his gaze a few seconds longer. Matt's heart quickened, and he smiled back.

He gingerly applied salve as he stared at her new hairdo. "It looks punk, but I like it."

Catherine flopped her head side to side, her hair swishing around her face. "Rock on! I never would have done anything this wild back in the old days. My parents would have freaked."

"Mine too," Matt said softly.

Everyone grew quiet, remembering their families and their loved ones.

"You look radical, like a member of The Clash or something!" Matt said, trying to turn things around before everyone broke down in tears. "We should all go."

The group followed Matt out of the Sev.

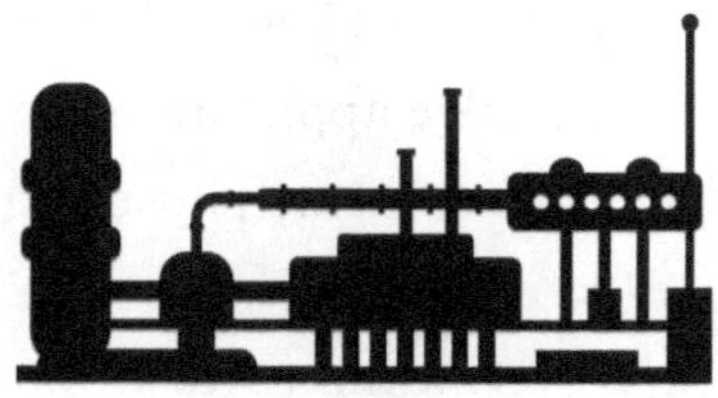

CHAPTER 4

At the edge of the big hole, they all glanced down into the dark.

"What did you find, chief?" Justin asked.

"Looks like we done found a basement in the woods," Cody said.

"This is, like, how horror movies start," Stacy added. "And I'm still stuck on your last name, Matt *Voorhees*."

Justin chortled. "We're already in a horror movie."

"What happened here?" Catherine gestured at the chasm.

"Darin's belt bomb," Matt said.

"Westbrook's, not mine," Darin broke in with a huff.

Matt nodded. "Right, Dr. Westbrook's bomb blasted a hole through . . . whatever."

"Maybe it's part of another base? Like maybe there's a C-85 or something," Catherine said as she leaned forward.

Matt grabbed onto her good shoulder to make sure she didn't lean too far in.

"This looks really dangerous, Matt," she said.

"It'll be all right," he said, guiding her back away from the edge and showing her his rope.

"I can't see the bottom, chief," Justin said. "Maybe this isn't such a good idea."

"That's what I said." Darin waved his hands.

Matt wrapped the end of the rope around the small steps of the cabin nearby.

"How are you even going to be able to tell if it reaches the bottom?" Catherine bit her lip, her eyebrows meeting to form a concerned V.

Matt gave her a friendly smile, doing his best Han Solo impression. "Trust me."

Catherine frowned.

"It'll be safe," he continued. "I want to get to the mountain and find our parents as much as anyone, but there's something down here that could get us out of all the weather. It could be safer."

"So how can you even test it?" Catherine asked.

"Simple." Matt took the end of the rope and hunted for a moment along the ground. When he found a good-sized quartz rock from the old Camp New Beginnings path, he wrapped it in a basket knot at the end of the rope. "I learned this in Scouts."

"A weighted end?" Catherine asked.

"If this touches bottom, we'll know the rope reaches the bottom safely," Cody said as Matt tossed the rope-knotted rock into the pit. The rope was pulled violently into the shaft, driven by the weight. The rough material slid through Matt's palms, threatening to chew them raw. He wished he had gloves. Just as he thought his hands would burst into flames, the clang of stone hitting metal sounded far below.

"How long is that rope?" Justin asked, looking at what was left of it coiled behind Matt.

"Almost two hundred feet," Cody replied. "I ain't never swung down anything that long before."

"I haven't either," Matt said, as he pulled the rope back up, "and without rappelling gear, this will be tricky. But I've got you guys to help me."

The end of the rope, minus the rock, plopped over the edge onto the ground next to the hole.

"Hey, where did your rock go?" Stacy asked.

"I think it broke when it hit bottom and came out of my knot," Matt said.

Justin shook his head. "What if it fell out of your knot, and you only thought it reached the bottom?"

"Don't worry about that. I'm positive it reached. I'll keep my feet cradled in the knot, and you guys lower me down and pull me back up."

"This will take everyone helping out except Stacy," Darin said with finality.

Catherine looked at Stacy, who only gave her a coy cock of the head.

Stacy brushed Darin's arm with her fingers and mouthed, "Thank you."

"Found these in the Sev." Cody shrugged, holding out a pair of walkie-talkies.

"Better hold onto this in case we can't hear you very good down there." Darin handed one of them to Matt.

Matt inspected the eight-inch, black, brick-style walkie-talkie with two dials on the face. He and his best friend,

Jed, used to play with them when they would dress up in camo gear. He clipped it to his belt opposite the hand-crank flashlight and nodded his thanks.

"You mean we aren't just going to go with one tug on the rope means 'lower me down,' and twenty-two tugs means 'I have to make a pit stop,' and sixty-six tugs means 'pull me up now'?" Justin taunted.

Catherine scowled at him as he chuckled at his own joke.

Matt ignored him and prepared to be lowered into the hole, keeping one foot in his knot-basket and the other leg free to kick himself off from the torn-open sides of the pit.

"Hey, Stacy, you be in charge of talking to Matt." Darin handed her the other walkie-talkie.

For at least six feet, there was exposed dirt and rocks with a healthy section of roots splayed at the edges of the hole. "Okay," Matt said to himself. "A good old dirt hole so far." A bit of dirt and dust trickled down beside him as he gingerly descended. A jagged patch of dried lava reminded him of last night's devastation.

"Real easy on this first part," Matt said. "Just exposed ground from the bomb blast." He looked up. "Something changed. The dirt's gone."

His stomach rolled nervously. Had this been the right idea? Was it as safe as he'd assured the others? Was there really anything to be learned from this basement in the woods?

CHAPTER 5

Surrounded by the darkness of the pit, Matt looked up toward his friends and clicked on the walkie. "Hey, what's happening up there?"

"He's confused. He needs help. Pull him out!" Stacy said.

Matt yelled, "No! No, I'm fine. Everything's okay."

Darin leaned over the hole, looked Matt in the eye, and shook his head. "Keep lowering him down. He's fine."

Bits of dirt and vegetation debris rained down on Matt. Some of it fell past his collar into his shirt. He shivered.

Once he reached about twenty feet down, Matt pushed the button on the walkie-talkie. "Breaker one-nine, breaker one-nine, this here is the Rubber Duck. What's happening topside? Over."

"I love *Smoky and the Bandit*," Stacy answered. "Over."

"I'm talking about *Convoy*," Matt corrected.

"Oh yeah, I knew that," she said with a giggle. "'East-bound and down, loaded up and trucking.' Over."

"That's still *Smoky and the Bandit*, but what I want to know is what is the weather like up there? I'm asking because I'm starting to hear something down here like gears moving and machines. Maybe fans starting up. I don't know."

"You've got to say 'over.' Over," Stacy reminded him.

"Over, Stacy, what is the weather like up there? Over."

"It's nice still. Did you find anything? Over."

"Not yet, have them keep sending me down."

Matt slid farther down, keeping one leg free to kick away from the edge. But after another slow twenty feet, his other leg grew restless, so he had his friends stop lowering him while he carefully switched his legs to keep the stationary one from going to sleep.

The clanking of machines grew louder, and a sudden blast of wind from below sent Matt crashing into the side wall. His cheek pressed against cool metal, and his heart raced with the thought of now being slammed into the other side by the buffeting wind.

"Are you okay, Matt? Over." Stacy's voice crackled through the walkie-talkie.

"I'm doing okay," Matt said. "Just a blast of wind or something. It kinda scared me for a second, and I hit the wall."

"Yeah, it startled us too. Over," Stacy said.

"Darin here. Did you say you hit the bottom?"

"No, I hit the side wall of the shaft."

"You guys need to be saying 'over,'" Stacy reminded them.

Matt shook his head at Stacy's observance of walkie-talkie protocol during an apocalypse. His heart leapt once more as his foot touched down on metal. He took the flashlight and cranked the knob a few times to get some light.

He hadn't reached the bottom, but rested on top of a thick chunk of grate, barring him from going down farther.

The rope went slack, as he was now fully standing on top of thick, crisscrossed metal bars.

"Hold on a minute. Over," he said.

"What happened?" Darin asked. "Did you find the bottom right after you said you didn't?"

"Not quite, hang on," Matt replied.

"Over," Stacy chirped.

The flashlight needed to be continually pumped, or the light faded quickly. He aimed the weak beam of light downward. A wide chunk of the grating had been eaten away by the lava from the night before. It was black and caked in the corner, but there was a big hole in the grating that he could continue down if he squeezed.

"I can keep going down, but I'll have to move where I'm at a bit. You guys probably ought to rearrange where you're lowering me from, too. It's a tight squeeze." He paused a moment before adding, "Over."

"Hold on." Darin's voice crackled through the walkie-talkie. "Are you saying the hole got smaller, and you want to keep going? I think that's a bad idea, dude. Too dangerous."

"No, the hole didn't get smaller. There's a grating over the shaft, but lava ate away at a section, and I can get through and keep going. It's all right."

"So you want to keep going down into a hole where you have to worm through a spot that lava opened up?"

"Yeah, it reminds me of the sarlacc pit that Boba Fett went into," Matt said.

"Boba Fett died in the sarlacc pit, chief," Justin said into the walkie-talkie.

"No, he didn't. In the comic, he climbed back out," Matt argued.

"Dude, I never saw *Jedi*, but climbing into a monster pit is not a good argument, no matter how you put it," Darin said.

"I read that issue," Cody said. "He went back into the sarlacc pit while fighting Han Solo, driving the Jawas' sand crawler. I think he died that second time."

"Okay. Bad analogy," Matt answered. "Over?" He angrily depressed the handle on the flashlight to keep looking around.

"We're gonna pull you up," Darin said. "This is way too dangerous."

"No, hang on." Matt stomped his foot in anger, and the grating beneath his feet fell away into the abyss. His stomach lurched, and he choked back a startled scream as he dropped about five feet before the rope went taut, holding him firm. The flashlight tumbled away in the dark, the light fading as the charge wore out as it followed the grating. The chunk of metal struck something below, the booming crash echoing through the darkness, followed by the crack of the flashlight breaking as it hit the ground. Disturbingly similar to what he imagined his bones breaking would sound like.

"What was that? Matt?!" Darin shouted into the walkie-talkie.

"I'm all right, just got seriously spooked. The grating fell to the bottom. I won't have to squeeze around it now."

"But you're okay?"

"Yeah, just about soiled my pants, but I'm all right."

"We'll bring you up."

"No. I really think I need to see what's at the bottom. There's something down there that the grate hit. Sounded like metal. It's only about another fifty feet. I'm just past halfway, I think. Let's finish this."

There was a long pause as the people at the top must have been discussing what to do.

"Cody says he's worried the rope is getting frayed, but if you really think this is something we should check out, I lost the vote," Darin said.

"Yes, I want to get to the bottom and investigate, so long as the weather above is holding out."

Darin sighed. "It's as nice as it's ever been, so yeah, but let's be quick about this, huh?"

"Agreed. Over," Matt said.

They gradually lowered him farther into the dark. He swung back and forth ever so slightly, like a pendulum.

The light from above was like a vague, square-shaped moon overhead. It gave light, but not enough to really see anything below. He found himself looking up toward it, then being blinded once he looked back down into the gloom.

His free foot traced along the slick edge of the metal shaft. Then it pressed against nothing but air.

Was he out of the abyss and into the antechamber below? He reminded himself to not look up at the opening so as not to become night-blind again.

"Hold up a minute. Let me see where I'm at. Over," Matt said into the walkie-talkie

"Thanks," Stacy said. "Over."

His eyes had to be playing tricks on him. Shadows coalesced out of the darkness. Forms moved and took the shape of wheels within wheels as the grinding of machinery creaked far away. Lights blinked in the distance—first white and then, farther away, red. They flashed everywhere to his right and his left.

After a moment, he realized he could see well down there, the same as if it were a starry night at home.

"Guys, I think you all better get down here. Over."

CHAPTER 6

In the eerie electric glow of the dim lights, Matt stared at enormous gears slowly turning like water wheels, flickering white lights off in the distance, blinking red lights on top of power boxes with coils of power cables stretching into infinity, pistons chugging up and down, and hydraulics pumping like heartbeats. "Everything is man-made," he said to himself.

He gazed in astonishment at the vastness of the place. "Guys, I think I'm in a building!" Matt yelled. He dangled and twirled slowly, eyes adjusting to the darker subfloor.

"Just like the Well of Souls where the Ark of the Covenant rested," Matt whispered to himself.

Not more than ten feet away was a catwalk and railing, the human highway for this place. If he swung hard enough, could he reach it and get a foothold?

"Catherine said she heard you shouting. Use the walkie-talkie," Darin reminded him. "Over."

Matt fumbled with the radio. "You guys need to see this. Get down here."

Darin's voice crackled over the walkie-talkie. "Why on earth should we do that?"

"Simple. This bunker is massive. I'm talking it has to be city blocks big. I can't see the end of it."

"Come again? Over?"

"You guys need to get down here and take a look at all of this. It's a whole big complex that stretches on and on. I'm seeing big gears and machines, cables and pumps, and electrical conduits. This is so big. It makes sense why nothing up on top is normal. There's something going on down here. Like maybe the underground vaults are way bigger than we thought."

"They are big," Darin answered, "but not as big as you're saying. Trust me."

"Trust *me* and come down here and see for yourself. I think there are machines down here running the weather and stuff up there. All of you need to come down and see it, now!" Matt snapped. "This is so crazy! Just like out of a sci-fi movie. Listen, I think these machines are running everything up there. I really think it'll be better down here. No natural disasters could touch us." It was unbelievable. The catwalk stretched on as far as he could see in either direction. Massive gears and pulleys groaned in the distance as cables and light fixtures sparked dully.

"Going down a rope is one thing. What about coming back up?" Darin asked.

"This place is so big, there have to be multiple exits farther down. Heck, maybe it even connects to the cryovault."

"No way," Darin broke in. "That's gotta be way too far."

"You guys have got to see this place. It's probably safer traveling down here than up there anyway. It's so big. This air vent is not the entrance. There must be lots of doors somewhere else."

"We'll put it to a vote," Darin said. "Give us a minute."

Matt waited in the dark. The flickering lights played with his senses. In another time and place, they might have been fireflies at night or the dim red light of someone's boom box playing music at a block party. But no, he was inside the vast dominion of a machine, something man-made and secret. A government bunker of sorts to protect mankind during the worst thing to hit the planet since the dinosaurs were annihilated.

Darin broke the silence with his walkie-talkie response. "It makes sense with an air vent that big that there must be a huge complex down there. I never saw anything like that when I was with Westbrook, but there are plenty of places he didn't let me go and see. It seems like it should tie into the Sev, but everyone here is excited to go and see it, so we'll come down."

"I think we're finally going to get some answers," Matt said.

CHAPTER 7

They eased Matt down another foot. He reached for the catwalk but couldn't quite get a hold. He said into the walkie-talkie, "Let me get my footing on the causeway and then you guys will have an easier time coming down after me. I'm going to need to swing a bit, back and forth, to reach it. Over."

"Copy that," Darin said.

"Be careful. Over," Stacy said.

Matt swung in the cradle with his free leg. It reminded him of using a regular swing, except now he only used one leg to pump back and forth to get momentum to move him closer and closer to the catwalk.

As his swing widened, he noted that the rope would occasionally pinch above him as it hit the corner where the shaft met the ceiling. It wouldn't stop him from swinging and reaching his goal, but it did make things a little harder. He had to pump extra hard to keep the momentum going.

"We're holding on to you really good," Darin said through the walkie-talkie.

Matt appreciated that but couldn't respond as he worked his leg back and forth. He was so close, but the walkway remained just out of reach. Another foot and he could grasp it with his free hand.

Almost making it was more demoralizing than realizing he could never make it at all. He had to work at keeping the swing going because the rope rubbing on the corner above was stealing his pendulum power. Finally, he concluded he could not reach the elevated steel path from this position. He got back on the walkie-talkie. "New plan, guys."

"Pull you back up?" Darin asked.

"No, maybe lower me another five feet. I need just a little more slack to reach it, since the rope keeps hitting the ceiling corner where the antechamber and the shaft meet."

"So down just another five feet?"

"Yeah, I think that will do it. Over."

"Roger that," Darin said.

Matt heard Justin in the background while the button was still depressed. "Ask him if he ever saw the movie *C.H.U.D.* and if he sees any down there?"

"What is a Chud?" Darin asked.

Then there was silence again as they left Matt to attempt his stunt.

Matt had seen *C.H.U.D.* but didn't want to think about any cannibalistic humanoid underground dwellers right now. He had to concentrate on grabbing the edge of the suspended walkway. And as he reached for the cold metal rail, it didn't help to think that a green-faced monster-man might try to sink blood-stained teeth into the back of his hand.

He swung back and forth, now able to pump his leg easier. But with more length, he now had to reach up above his head to grasp the iron railing.

He strained and caught the lowest rung of the causeway's safety rail with his right hand and held on for all he was worth. He struggled to grasp the walkie-talkie with his left hand and depress the button to talk. "Hey, guys, I've got it, but need you to pull me up a little so I can climb up. Over."

"Understood. Over," Stacy said. "Guys, pull him up a few feet."

Matt expected them to pull the rope a couple of feet. Instead, they yanked him up six feet. He flew end over end, and his foot came loose of the knot.

He fell, gravity pulling him down, the rope out of reach.

"Ah!" Matt screamed.

He flailed his arms, but there was nothing to grab on to. The walkway he had struggled so hard to get to became his lifeline as his hand made contact with the metal handrail just as his body slammed into the side of the suspended path.

"Are you okay?" Darin shouted into the walkie-talkie. "We just pulled a little, and all your weight is gone! Are you all right? Matt. Matt. Matt!"

Catherine's garbled shouts came from far above. "Matt! Are you okay? Did you fall?"

Matt couldn't depress the button to respond. The

walkie-talkie was the last thing on his mind as he threw all his energy into holding on to the causeway. The whole thing swayed as he pulled up and threw a leg over the handrail. Had the floods, avalanches, and volcanic eruptions destroyed its stability?

Scratchy voices continued spouting from the walkie-talkie in a chaotic cacophony as the others argued over what to do.

Matt got his foot over the side, then struggled to move his entire body to the cold metal floor. He took a deep breath, fully realizing how close he had come to death, then grasped the walkie-talkie. "I made it, guys."

"You're all right?" Catherine asked.

"Yes, just catching my breath. Give me a minute to find something to snag the rope with, and I'll secure it for you guys to come down."

"Are you sure that's a good idea, Matt?" Stacy questioned.

Glancing down the catwalk, he found a spare piece of a crossbeam from a pile of scaffolding. It was awkward, but he slung it over the edge of the causeway, reached the dangling rope, and let it slide down the piece of scaffolding into his waiting hands.

Back on the walkie-talkie, Matt said, "All right, guys, you're good to go. Come on down."

CHAPTER 8

"Can you see any better down there now?" Darin asked.

"Yeah, it's like a big subbasement, maybe ten stories down."

"Okay," Darin said over the walkie-talkie.

"I think I *am* in a building!" Matt exclaimed. "You gotta come see this. That means this is so big, we can go all the way to the mountain. There's a tram track next to the catwalk I'm on. I think we can take that. I've tied the rope onto the edge of the metal railing. So as long as you guys go slow and easy, you can get right to where I am, no sweat."

There was a pause, and then Darin answered back, "All right, we all agreed that it may be the best way to go. Less natural disasters. More protected, if you know what I mean. No more obstacles to survive. It might be a lot better to go to the mountain from down there."

Matt clapped his hands together. He truly believed they would have a much better chance walking down in a creepy industrial basement than out there in the crazy apocalyptic weather. "Great, who's coming down first?"

"Stacy is. Cody has rigged up a harness to help us get down. We'll all help ease each other down, and I'll go last since I can just climb down myself," Darin said.

"All right, let her rip," Matt responded as he got ready to help Stacy once she reached the railing.

It took longer than he expected, but it was a lot to ask of people who had never done anything like this before. How many other teens had slid down a rope, hundreds of feet, into a dark pit inside what must be a gigantic underground bunker?

The rope jerked a little as Stacy was eased down, her legs clasped about it and her arms held in a harness.

"This does not feel good. My arms are gonna get pulled from the sockets. Am I almost there, Matt?"

"Yes. Almost. Just a few more feet, then you need to let go of the rope with your shoes and touch down on the top of the railing. I've got you."

"Okay," she said reluctantly.

She started to move one leg from the rope, then hesitated, squeezing her eyes shut and clamping her legs tighter around the lifeline.

"Let me help you." Matt took a gentle hold of Stacy's uninjured foot and guided it to the railing. "Now you're touching the catwalk. I've got you; you can climb on down now."

She gingerly reached out and put her hands on his shoulders as he eased her down. As soon as she stood solidly on the catwalk, balancing most of her weight on her unburned foot, she pulled her arms out of the harness and exhaled a big breath of air. "That wasn't so bad—for a horror movie."

Matt got back on the walkie-talkie. "Stacy is down, and we're good. Go ahead and have Catherine come down."

The rope harness disappeared back up the hole. They took turns, and soon enough, both Catherine and Justin had made it. Matt continued to help each person down as the others moved along the catwalk a short distance to take in the bizarre imagery of the underground facility.

"Which way should we go?" Justin asked.

"To the left." Stacy stood facing him and Catherine.

"Which left?" Justin asked. "Ours or yours?"

"It's always the left of the person who said it," Catherine said.

"But she pointed right!"

"That's what I said!" Stacy exclaimed.

Cody descended next, hand over hand, nice and quick. He still had the harness over his arms, but he made the journey on his own power with Darin holding the rope above as insurance.

"Whew! Now that was a whole rodeo in and of itself," Cody said as he reached the catwalk and jumped down. He took off the harness and tugged on the rope so Darin would know to pull it back up the shaft.

"You gonna be all right coming down on your own?" Matt asked Darin over the walkie-talkie.

"I'll be fine. I'll come down just like Cody did. Just gotta reconfigure this rope. I've got an idea on how to keep it."

"Keep it?" Matt asked.

"Yeah, I think if I loop it around the cabin's front posts, and you keep your end tied to the railing, I'll tie this end around me, take up all the slack, and lower myself down," Darin explained.

Matt agreed. "Then we can pull it to us. Like top-roping. Yeah. I learned that in Scouts. The rope would be great to have."

"Good thing you got a long rope," Darin said. "I'm reattaching it to the cabin, and I should be able to start sliding down here shortly."

CHAPTER 9

Darin began his journey down the shaft with a joke over the walkie-talkie. "Hey, you guys!"

"Be careful!" Catherine cautioned.

The rope whipped back and forth as Darin made his way down, shouting, "Ruth! Ruth! Baby! Ruth!"

Catherine furrowed her brow. "Is he making *Goonies* references? Someone already used that a few days ago."

Matt shrugged. "Yeah, he hasn't seen as many movies as us. I think he's trying to fit in a little more."

"Stop messing around, and just get down here," Stacy shouted.

"I'm coming," Darin shouted back, no longer worrying about using the walkie-talkie. "I've just got to—"

Darin's legs slipped from around the rope, dumping all of his weight onto his hands as they gripped it. Sliding fast, his feet hit the metal railing, snapping the bars and sending him flying into the abyss.

Matt and Cody lunged, grabbing his arms and shirt to

pull him up over the broken railing. Catherine took hold of the back of his pants to help hoist him over.

"We've got you!" Matt gasped as they yanked him back to the causeway. They all sighed in unison, relief evident on their faces.

"Are you hurt?" Catherine asked.

Darin shook his hands. "My hands." He opened and closed them, examining the raw palms.

"Did we bring Stacy's burn cream?" Matt asked.

"I did." Darin gestured to his backpack. "It's back there."

Catherine reached into his pack and pulled out the burn cream. After applying it to Darin's hands, she gingerly wrapped them with gauze and athletic tape. "You're good to go. Kinda."

"I'll say. I won't be climbing back up that thing anytime soon." Darin squinted up at the rope.

"Well," Catherine said, "if we have to go back that way, we'll all pull you up like you let us down."

"I—I'm sorry. I didn't mean to let you down," Darin said.

"You know what I mean." She rolled her eyes.

Darin smiled.

Cody changed the subject. "You know, guys, this dang walkway is as rickety as the axle on my grandpa's tractor."

Matt grimaced. "Yeah. Let's get going. Get off of this section. A chunk of grating hit the whole thing when I came down too."

"Which way should we go?" Cody asked.

"I think east," Matt said.

"How can you know which way is east, chief?" Justin taunted.

Matt pointed to the catwalk. Spray painted in faint yellow paint were two arrows, followed by the word "east," with the letters stacked the length of the walkway.

Justin smiled. "Okay, smart-ass. I didn't see that."

Matt clapped Justin on the back. "It's okay, buddy."

"All right," Darin said. "Let's go that way. Bring the rope."

"Good idea," Cody chimed in.

Matt pulled the rope until all of it came tumbling down. He coiled it up and slung it over his shoulder.

"You ready to go, camp counselor?" Justin patted Darin on the shoulder.

Darin nodded, his lips drawn tight against his teeth as he clenched his bandaged hands.

They walked along the catwalk a quarter-mile, taking in the surreal metallic jungle. Every fifty yards or so was a cage-covered sconce or a pendulum light that seemed to flicker at inopportune times, so they would just hold the railing as their guide to the next flickering bulb. Just to the side of the railing and walkway, there were stiff cables bolted into the ceiling. Tubes of gurgling water big enough to be a waterslide wound through scaffolding. Rusted ductwork blew air down on them. They were in an industrialized maze.

"That must've been one big rooster to lay an egg that big." Cody pointed to a curious, rounded dome in the ceiling ahead.

Large glass bulbs, as big as a small house, hung down like clear eggs, containing dark soil and the curling roots of trees that poked through the subfloor above. Beyond, huge rock pillars with man-sized pipes bolted to them stood like sentinels every few hundred feet, holding up the roof of the underground base.

Justin's eyes bulged. "What the what? The forest floor is the ceiling!"

Cody whistled. "This is way bigger than I thought."

"What is this place?" Stacy asked.

"We are definitely not in Kansas anymore," Matt said.

CHAPTER 10

"It looks like there's another, even bigger bulb up ahead," Cody said.

They moved a little faster, anxious to see what this unreal example of the underground world could be.

"That's not another tree in a pot." Darin pointed. "Look, it's like a sink basin, except we're seeing it from below. It's the lake!"

It, too, was made of clear glass or plastic. The higher shore had mud and rocks, but there were several spots without mud or sand where light shone through, as if the bottom was a dirty pool.

"It's all fake," Catherine gasped. "Nothing is real! Everything we thought about this world is man-made."

"Darin?" Matt questioned.

Darin narrowed his eyes, whispering, "I didn't know anything about this. I thought we were in the real world as much as you guys."

"What haven't you told me?" Matt pressed.

Stacy, standing beside Darin, stuck her tongue out at Matt.

Cody changed the subject. "There must be millions of yards of dirt above us to make a false forest."

"False everything," Catherine said bitterly.

"But how? Why?" Justin asked.

"*Why* is the best question." Darin craned his head around the incredibly huge perimeter beneath the lake.

Matt pointed at the collection of massive gears, huge tubes, and vents in the ceiling above them. "This reminds me of when my parents took us to the Universal Studios backlot tour. There were different movie scene places made to create atmosphere. Like we would go into a small South American city, and a flash flood would come racing toward the tour bus, but since it was fake, it never hit us. Then there was a subway area that simulated an earthquake, and a big fuel semitruck almost hits you, and the road collapses from above, and the fuel tanker slides toward you, and there's fire and water. But then everything resets."

"The tour has Jaws too, chief, so what?" Justin taunted.

"What I'm saying," Matt persisted, "is that this all reminds me of that. If everything here is a soundstage like for a movie, maybe that's how the cabins and trees reset after the avalanche. And how the water drained so quickly after the flood."

"It's not just a simulation, though. Our friends have died!" Catherine shouted, falling to her knees.

Stacy moved to help her up, but Catherine uncharacteristically pushed her away amidst sobs. "But why?" she cried. "Who is torturing us like this?!"

"I'd say Westbrook, but he's dead," Darin muttered.

"This has got to be bigger than just Westbrook," Matt said. "But if we keep going, we should find some answers." He leaned down and helped Catherine up, put his arms around her, and let her sob into his shoulder. "We'll get out of this, somehow."

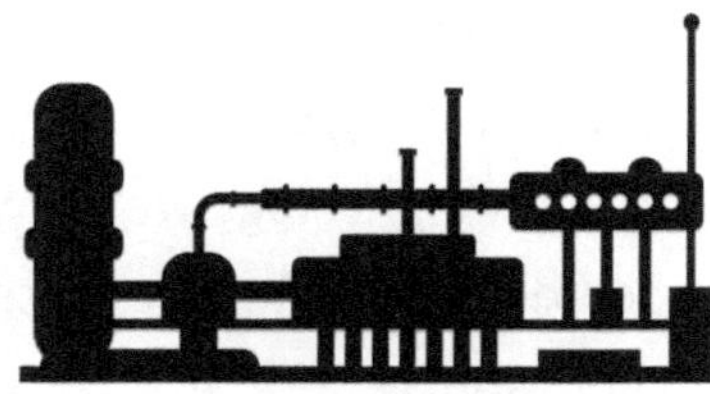

CHAPTER 11

The gloom of the humongous chamber was cast into further darkness as some of the dim light from the exposed sections of the lake basin above swirled and vanished.

"I think it's storming up there," Justin said. "Raining maybe."

"Or a hurricane," Stacy offered.

"Doubt that," Cody said.

"We're safe down here, for now," Darin assured her.

Catherine scowled. "It's all fake. Why would anyone do this to us?"

They watched the lake above cascade between bouts of moving water and glints of light from the surface.

Cody coughed, breaking the silence. "Matt, you said this is bigger than Westbrook. How can we know that?"

Matt held his hands out, gesturing to the massive volume of the underground facility. "Look at all this. Westbrook sure didn't do it by himself. He couldn't have. Plus, there was the apocalypse that had the government rallying to get people from everywhere cryogenically frozen to survive it all. This is so big, it had to have been built by hundreds, maybe thousands, of people, which took time and money."

"Lots of time," Darin said.

"Years and years." Justin nodded.

"How much money?" Stacy asked.

"Tons," Justin answered.

"So," Matt continued, "there have to be answers somewhere, and we have to find them."

"More than that." Catherine wiped at her tear-moistened face. "All the crazy weather that's killed our friends, some of it must have come from inside here. Maybe there's an on and off switch."

Darin opened his mouth as if to speak, but then shut it and looked down at his feet.

"What is it, Darin?" Matt asked.

Darin shook his head. "I thought I might know something, but I really don't."

"Well, what are your thoughts? Since you knew Westbrook and the cryovault better than any of us ever will," Matt prodded.

Darin put his hand on his forehead, as if he could wipe away a memory, but came away just shaking his head again. "I really don't know. I thought I had an idea, but I lost it."

"Oh, Lance-Darin." Stacy ran her hands over his shoulders affectionately.

"I like the idea of there being an on and off switch," Matt said. "These are all machines running and creating a false world above. There must be a control room."

"And if there's a control room, there must be some

answers!" Justin insisted. "I like where this is going, chief. Time for some payback!"

"There is no payback!" Catherine argued. "We just need to get out of here and find our families."

Matt stood between the two of them. "You're both right. We are going to get to the bottom of this mystery, find our parents, and hopefully get some justice."

"Where do we even start?" Stacy asked.

Cody looked up and down the causeway. "Well, we know what was back that way a good half mile or more. I say we see what farther down the line this way holds."

"I agree," Matt said. "I'm pretty sure this is taking us back the way we came in the truck when we all woke up. To the east."

"East? Are you sure?" Catherine asked.

"I sure think so. Besides, we're even deeper than the Sev here, so it makes sense that this might connect all the way to the mountain."

"Or it might not," Darin said. "I never saw anything like this back where I was with Westbrook. And we have no way of knowing for sure which way is east. Everything can get real mixed up down in a cave like this."

"But that doesn't mean it doesn't connect, either," Matt said.

"How can you know, Matt?" Catherine asked.

"I just have a good sense of direction."

"I trust you, Matt," Cody said.

"That's a big gamble," Justin said.

Matt closed his eyes and ran his hand over his short hair. "Every choice we have left is a gamble. This one seems safer than outside. I think if they built a warehouse in a cave, then the cave could be man-made as well. Just like this entire place we're seeing from a new perspective. We've already made the decision, so we need to carry on and go to the mountain."

"You're right," Darin relented. "I'm just not sure we'll be happy with any possible revelations we get from this place."

"Revelations? Like from the Bible?" Stacy asked.

"It *is* the apocalypse," Cody added with a wry grin.

"Oh geez, not with the Bible stuff again, cowboy," Justin said.

Darin looked at Stacy and pulled her close, his head over her shoulder.

"All right, you win, chief. We go the way you think the mountain is. You've been right about things so far." Justin gave Matt a warm slap on the back. "I'm trusting you about the man-made mountain inside the building. I guess the cave within a mountain must be man-made too."

"Thanks," Matt said, thinking the slap on the back was just a tad too hard to be sincere.

They walked on, water dripping somewhere in the dark, and rusted metal creaking under their feet.

"How old does this place look to you?" Matt asked Darin.

"I have no idea."

"It looks really old to me, like ancient history," Stacy said. "Maybe forty years."

There were cracks in some of the concrete pillars, along with mildew or algae growing along spots where it looked like water had leaked from above. The causeway had more rust, and the groaning of the metal became louder with each step.

"This does not sound good," Catherine said.

"We should probably space ourselves out a—" Cody's words were lost as the entire section of catwalk they were on collapsed.

Screams and curses echoed in the vast darkness.

CHAPTER 12

The rusted catwalk slammed hard against another walkway below. Bodies spilled over the top of each other from the terrible impact, careening head over heels. Justin, Catherine, and Stacy flew forward into a rectangular hole. Stacy caught herself on the far edge and managed to avoid falling like the other two into yet another dark chamber.

Matt glanced at where the two had disappeared and rushed over to help. Darin sprang into action moments after him.

"What in the *Donkey Kong*?" Matt muttered.

"Are they . . ." Cody asked as he peered down into the hole.

"Is anyone hurt?" Matt asked.

"My heart about exploded," Stacy said. "But nothing is broken."

"Thanks to me," Justin grumbled. "What did we land in?"

Big metal gears with teeth the size of cars rose on either side of them.

"Catherine is looking dizzy. She might have hit her head. Get us out of here!" Justin shouted.

Matt slid the coiled rope from his shoulder.

"Hurry!"

"Stacy?" Darin asked.

"I'm all right, now that you're here. Help me get back over to that side with you," she said.

Darin stretched his arm out but wasn't even close to reaching Stacy on the far side of the hole. "I can't reach her." He glanced about for help.

"What about you, Darin?" Matt asked as he unwound the rope.

"Just some bumps and bruises," he answered.

"I bit my tongue," Cody said as he came forward to help. "But at least we landed on another walkway. Coulda been real bad if we hadn't."

"It will get real bad down here if you don't hurry up," Justin called.

As if responding to his warning, a motorized rumbling began in the distance.

"Something is starting up!" Justin cried.

With a slight jerk, the massive teeth of the gears vibrated. Catherine and Justin were trapped in a gear box between teeth that were about to move.

"Hold on!" Matt unwound another section of rope and tossed the end down. "Put this around you and Catherine, and we'll pull you up!"

"Not gonna work, chief. We'd be too heavy, and she's

too out of it to hang on. I can't hold on to her and the rope."

"Then just you climb out!" Darin shouted amidst the growing cacophony of popping and buzzing as the machine continued to fire up. "We're running out of time!"

"I can't leave her!" Justin yelled.

Matt glanced about for what to do. Cody grabbed a broken section of railing and pulled on it. Matt guessed his intent and helped him yank on the rusted guard railing until it snapped from its housing.

Shaped almost like a piece of a ladder, they lowered it down to Justin, who caught the end and braced it against the top of a gear section. It was still a couple of feet short of the top, but if he stood on it, he could reach the others to climb out.

A loud hiss of steam blasted from a vent nearby.

"Hurry!" Stacy screamed.

Justin roused Catherine and guided her to the rickety, makeshift ladder. She seemed groggy, but followed his lead and climbed up the rungs one by one. When she got as high as she could, Matt and Darin reached down, took her by the wrists, and pulled her up.

A loud popping and a final snap indicated the gear was moving. The rickety, broken railing skittered as the gear moved beneath it. Justin raced up the rungs and caught the top of the box just as the gears forced the railing to drop between the teeth. The machinery chewed and pulled the twisted bit of metal until it vanished between the enormous gears like the final slurp through a straw.

Justin launched himself up over the side, landing at the feet of the others.

He lay on the floor of the causeway, gulping in air. "I thought that was it," he panted.

"You're a good man," Cody said.

"Huh?"

"You saved Catherine." Matt extended a hand.

"Yeah," Justin said, getting to his feet. "Had to. We've only got each other now."

Matt nodded but said, "Our families are still out there. We'll find them."

They used another piece of railing to help Stacy cross over and reach the safety of the catwalk. She burrowed into Darin's chest, stifling her sobs. He wrapped his arms around her, holding her tight.

"Hand me a flashlight." Matt turned to Catherine. "Let me see your eyes."

"Why?" she asked.

"I want to see if you have a concussion."

"How can you tell?" She blinked as Matt shined the light in her face.

"Your pupils aren't different sizes, and they react to the light, so I think that means you don't have a concussion."

"Well, small miracles, I guess," she said.

"In this place, I'd call it a big miracle." Justin frowned.

"I think we can use this piece to get back up to our original catwalk." Cody ripped off another piece of railing and leaned it like a ladder up against the section above, across from where they'd been before it snapped.

"Like, what if it falls again?" Stacy asked.

"I think it was just this part that was worn through. The rest doesn't look nearly as rusted," Cody assured her.

"Let's try it out. We need to keep moving," Matt said.

Cody went first, then Matt and Justin.

"It seems solid enough," Matt said.

Catherine rubbed her forehead, still dazed. "I can make it. Just hold it steady please."

Darin held the bottom firmly, and she climbed up, assisted by Matt when she neared the top.

Finally, Darin held it for Stacy, who went up with only minor difficulty due to her injured foot. Then Darin ascended, and they were ready to continue on their path.

"From now on, we'd better look at our feet as often as around us," he said.

CHAPTER 13

They left the lake basin and broken section of the causeway far behind them. Along the way, they saw more bulb-like projections denoting the bigger trees, and even portions of rock used as natural pillars to hold up the great forest floor.

A few machines looked to be running smoothly—like water pumps or even what looked like giant furnaces and air conditioners. Once in a while, they would see a machine that was clearly broken or had scorch marks, as if it had caught on fire. One section of pipe had a split at an elbow and leaked gallons of water every second. The water fell into the dark below, splashing into whatever was down there.

Matt guessed they had walked almost a half-mile when something new in the distance caught his eyes.

"What is that?" Catherine asked.

"Might be some kind of turbine or big air-conditioning box," he suggested.

"I'll tell you what that is, chief," Justin said with a chuckle.

"What?" Matt asked, curious as to how he could possibly know.

"That, my friend, is what I used to call home."

"Home? Here?" Catherine and Matt asked at the same time.

Justin shook his head. "No. I grew up dirt poor. That is a single-wide trailer. Must be used here as an engineer's office or something. They're easy to move, so they always get used as office trailers on construction sites. When they were building all of this, they must have used that to keep blueprints and work orders and stuff in."

"That means it might have information for us! Maybe a map!" Matt's voice rose with excitement.

He and Justin started to run ahead. "Hey, remember we gotta make sure the walkway isn't rusting out under our feet again!" Darin called to them.

They slowed and glanced at the causeway before deciding it was safe and rushing on.

The trailer was suspended on big cables attached to the ceiling. It was a single story, and except for this surreal location, it looked just as Justin had said, the perfect little portable office for a construction job site.

"Hang on, guys!" Darin called as he helped Stacy limp along, Catherine trailing slowly behind them. "Make sure those cables aren't rusted out."

Cody caught up to Matt and Justin and took it upon himself to investigate the far side of the trailer's support cables. "This side is good. No rust here at all."

"Not on this end either," Matt said.

"Well, let's go in. Anybody home?" Justin knocked on the door.

The thin metal door had a painted number four near the top. The doorknob was a standard silver, with a big keyhole taking up the center. Matt half expected it to be locked and was already wondering what they could use to break it open, when the handle turned easily in Justin's hand.

"It's dark," Cody said.

"Find the light switch," Matt said.

"It's over here, chief." Justin entered and flipped on the lights.

Matt and Cody cautiously followed him in. There were bookcases filled with rolled-up papers—probably blueprints—a pair of desks, a half-dozen chairs, a small fridge, and a wastepaper basket, all covered in a thick layer of dust.

Justin smiled. "Told you. There are lots of blueprints, kind of like back at the Sev."

Matt eyed the bookshelves. "Yeah, but a lot more."

They moved closer. The blueprints were marked "HZRD."

"That must mean that this is the HZRD site," Matt said.

Darin and the girls made it to the door. "I thought I asked you guys to wait up. We've gotta be careful."

"Just leave the injured one behind." Stacy crossed her arms and pushed her bottom lip out in a pout.

"Sorry," Matt said. "I just really wanted to see what was in here."

"Eager beaver," Catherine taunted.

"Look at these." Matt held out one of the blueprints for them all to see.

"Is that what I think it is?" Catherine asked. "It looks like the entire layout of the building. It's massive."

"More than massive. It's bigger than a city," he said.

Justin checked the fridge, grinning when he found a couple of cans of soda. He took one and reclined in one of the nicer chairs behind a desk. "Explain it to me, chief," he said, cracking open a can.

"Don't drink that. You don't know how old it is." Catherine screwed up her face in disgust.

Justin shook his head and lifted the can in salute. "Down the hatch."

"Is there any more?" Stacy asked.

Justin chugged the soda and pointed to the fridge. "Wow, that has a tang to it." He shivered as he swallowed again.

Darin and Matt looked at each other. "It can't be any older than the stuff in the Sev," Matt said.

"We don't know that," Catherine protested.

"Well, this should start giving us some answers." Matt pointed at marks on one of the blueprints.

"This is called the elevation of the blueprints of the building. So you can see what it looks like from the outside," Darin added.

Catherine pointed. "That enormous square looks like it has some little drawings of shrubs around a driveway to a door. What door?"

"To the outside—the *real* outside," Justin suggested with a hiccup.

"I was hoping we'd already reached the *real* outside,

just in part of a big underground base," Cody said. "I mean, who in the world could make anything so dang big?"

"The government, apparently. But why?" Catherine said.

Darin pointed at different areas on the paper. "The blueprints have a bird's-eye view, which is typical. This shows both the ground level and the subfloor. That's where we are, down here. Over there, it shows the walkways, and over there is where the mountain is."

"So that's the cryovault where our parents are!" Matt almost shouted.

Darin kept going. "This shows a tram system and a track. Looks like a direct route to get there from here. You were right about wanting to come down here."

"Thank you," Matt said with a slight bow.

Catherine touched the blueprint. "Look! There's the forest, and next to it is Camp New Beginnings, and there's the Sev."

"Hang on a sec, I just found the size calculator for this thing," Matt said. There was a line and four hash marks in the lower part of the blueprint. His lips moved as he counted to himself and measured the diameter of the blueprint. "This is incredible. It's way bigger than I thought."

"How big?" Cody asked.

Matt held his arms out wide. "This thing is over forty-five miles in diameter."

"It's a fortress," Justin said.

"It's a city," Stacy added.

"It's bigger than a city." Darin shook his head.

"It's, like, bigger than Rhode Island!" Stacy shrugged. "I mean, probably!"

Catherine pointed to marks on the blueprint. "This shows where all the tram stations are. If the trams are running, we can ride to the mountain. No more walking for dizzy people or anyone with a bad foot." She put an arm around Stacy.

"Awww," Stacy cooed, embracing Catherine back.

"No more walking for anyone," Justin added with a smile as he cracked another can open.

"How about saving one for someone else?" Cody asked.

"I waited. Nobody else grabbed one." Justin took a gulp.

Matt took charge. "Guys. We know that the cryovault is B-35, but nothing is marked B-35 on this blueprint. But I think the mountain probably *is* the cryovault, isn't it?"

"I would think so," Darin said. "I saw it from the outside once."

"You did?" Stacy gasped.

Darin hung his head. "Yeah, but just once."

"I also think we need to find a way out of this place. These are all labeled HZRD, but nothing says B-35. What if it's not even in this giant building? What is the exit for a building this big?" Catherine asked.

"I think the tram stations will route us to exits. They had to have them when they built this place," Darin said.

"These marks on the edge look like exits to me." Matt gestured at the blueprint.

"We take the tram, find the mountain, and find an exit," Cody summarized.

"Exactly what I said," Justin proclaimed.

"So we're in agreement?" Matt asked. "We take the tram to the mountain, find our parents, and get out of here?" Everyone agreed with a nod. "All right, let's get moving!"

CHAPTER 14

"I'm taking these, since nobody has been here in ages." Matt rolled up the blueprints to put in his backpack.

"How long do you think it's been since someone has been here?" Stacy asked.

"Anyone who worked on this place is probably long since dead," Justin said.

"Morose much?" Catherine fixed him with her gaze.

"Hey, look at the dust in here. How long do *you* think it's been since anyone has been here?" Justin prodded. "Probably like twenty years or more."

"I'm sure I don't know," she answered. "How was your soda?"

"Good." Justin wiped his sleeve across his mouth for emphasis. "It's a dead man's soda. Who could ask for more? Don't run away. It's only me," he sang as he moved with arms outstretched, Frankenstein-like, toward Catherine.

"Stop it!" she said with a slight smile.

Matt was glad she seemed to be overcoming her breakdown from earlier.

"Wait, if this is like a map," Cody said, "how do we know where we are, though?"

"Already covered," Matt said. "This building is marked four on the door, and right in the dead center—"

"Don't say dead," Catherine cautioned as Justin continued his "dead man's soda" chant.

Matt shook his shoulders. "This trailer is labeled four, and I found a four on the blueprint right here in the middle. So the closest tram is just over here. Looks like less than a half-mile walk."

"I'm glad you understand that thing," Cody said.

"Do you think the tram still works?" Stacy asked. "I'm tired of walking like this."

"Lean on me." Darin put an arm around her shoulders.

They followed Matt as he pointed down one of several causeways leading in multiple directions.

Justin burped loudly, rather pleased with himself.

"Ugh, excuse you," Catherine said. "That echoed in my ears like a gong down here."

"That part wasn't me. There's some kind of banging up ahead," Justin said.

Along the causeway to their right, in the direction Matt had indicated, the noise grew. The ever-louder sounds rattled like an engine tugging against its support brackets to their left, and to the right, the noisy clanking of a vent banging against itself blasted their ears in stereo.

"That does not sound good," Catherine said.

"Sounds like they're still doing construction down

here. I need earplugs." Stacy wrapped her hoodie around her head tight and covered her ears with her hands.

They passed by one of the vents slamming against itself. They could hardly hear each other speak, and Matt shouted for them to pick up the pace and get away from the noise.

Cody held his hands over his ears and tripped a little on a raised bar on the causeway, bumping into Matt. "Sorry."

"What?"

"I'm sorry."

Matt nodded as they covered their ears again.

Catherine tugged on Matt and shouted, "I'm beginning to think we went the wrong way!"

Matt shook his head and showed her the blueprints, shouting, "No, this is the right way. We're almost there!"

"What?"

"Just follow me!"

CHAPTER 15

They moved on and came to a walled section. Passing through the doorway, moving tubes came into view, and the constant drumming of machines pounded their ears.

"What are those?" Stacy asked.

"Looks like tubes?" Catherine answered.

The walkway curved like a big letter Z as it made its way through a section of massive pistons pumping up and down. Some of the larger ones were almost ten feet in diameter, and as tall as trees. Matt had never seen machines this big before, but considering the massive gears and other works down there, he wasn't surprised they existed. The noise eased slightly, but still pounded in his head.

"What the heck are these doing?" Stacy asked.

"They're pistons, like in a car engine," Cody said.

"Yeah, but what are they doing? Is this whole place moving somewhere now?" she asked.

Darin smiled at her. "Who knows? These must be pumping or powering something. I don't know what—

maybe an air venting system or moving water from up above.”

“It’s an industrial forest of working trees,” Cody said. “We have plenty of oil derricks out where I live, and these might be doing something similar to that.”

“Like collecting the fuel to run this place?” Catherine asked.

“Maybe. This base is so big, it must take crazy amounts of gas to run everything—electric generators and water pumps, air vents, even sewage maybe.” Cody shrugged.

“Nobody uses pistons to move sewage.” Justin laughed. “Pistons power motors, but if you don’t add oil, they seize up, and your engine blows.”

“Well, I’m glad it looks like these are oiled, then,” Catherine said.

“That one isn’t moving.” Stacy pointed to a single piston that remained still.

“You spoke too soon,” Justin said. “Now we’re in trouble.”

The stalled piston shuddered as it struggled to move.

Stacy paused on the walkway, and Darin rushed to reassure her. “It looks like it’s seized, but it’s not gonna blow up. Just, this place is old, and some things don’t work anymore. It’s okay. Let’s keep moving.”

She shivered. “I don’t like this place anymore. I want to get out of here and see the sun again.”

“We haven’t seen the sun for a long time,” Justin answered.

“You’re not helping,” Catherine chided.

"We are getting out," Darin said calmly. "We're on our way to get out."

"So maybe those things power bad weather outside?" Stacy asked.

"Looks that way, and maybe if they aren't working anymore, weather will be better," Darin said.

"Well, I want all the way out of this madhouse." Justin gestured to their surroundings.

Matt broke in, trying to end the talk scaring Stacy. "We're on our way, guys. We'll get there."

The pistons continued their heartbeat-like action, and as they followed the walkway through the metal forest, someone dropped something. It skidded on the metal grating and then tumbled off the edge.

"What was that?" Matt asked.

"I dropped one of my snacks," Justin said. "I didn't hear it hit bottom."

Cody leaned over the side of the walkway and pumped his flashlight, aiming the beam of light below them. Matt moved in beside him to get a look too.

The pistons sunk way down into the ground, sliding up and down, with thick brown sludge around the junction of the compressing rod and the outer housing.

"We're higher up than I thought," Matt said.

"What do you mean?" Catherine asked.

"I thought the walkway here was like twenty feet off the floor, but I'd say we're more like over a hundred feet up."

"Are we still on the right path? I thought a tram station would be closer," she said.

"So did I," he lamented. "It's gotta be up here soon."

A hiss from far below echoed through the chamber, adding to the screeching of mechanical pumping. The sound was an ominous rhythm daring them to walk forward.

CHAPTER 16

"Maybe we took a wrong turn?" Catherine suggested.

Matt looked at the blueprint again. "I'm pretty sure I led us the right way. It shouldn't be much farther, but it does seem strange that there wasn't a more direct route to the tram from supervisors' section four."

"We all make mistakes, chief. You just make more," Justin joked.

"Thanks a lot for all your help." Matt gritted his teeth.

"You're welcome. So do we turn back or keep going?" Justin pressed.

"I still think we're on the right track to the nearest tram. I can't explain why they built it like this. Maybe they thought workmen would be running diagnostic checks on things as they walked between spots?" Matt suggested.

"That makes sense to me," Cody said. "You always gotta ride your fences to make sure things are on the up and up."

"Yeah, yeah, you two are always backing each other up." Justin glowered at them.

"It's not like that." Catherine moved to catch up to Justin, who was now in the lead moving down the walkway. Darin and Stacy followed after, while Matt paused a moment.

"Don't take none of that personal," Cody said. "We're all pushed to our limits down here."

Matt couldn't hear very well amidst the barrage of pistons pumping, but he could see Catherine talking to Justin as they walked ahead of the others. He was grateful she was such a good friend with a level head. Even after her breakdown earlier at the realization of their strange predicament, she seemed to be overcoming it for the good of all of them.

There was a loud pop, and Catherine screamed, racing back toward the others, Justin on her heels.

A black hose whipped back and forth, snakelike, spraying hot hydraulic fluid, drenching them all in the slick substance.

Matt struggled to cover the blueprints with his body, then stuffed them into his pack while getting sprayed.

"It's not stopping!" Catherine cried.

"We have to go that way. Let's run past it!" Matt shouted.

"No, let's find another way," Darin said.

"No other route was even close to this short," Matt protested.

"Can you run?" Darin asked Stacy.

She shook her head.

"I've got you." Darin picked her up and rushed to get past the spraying hose.

They all ducked and crawled and slipped their way past the angry, mindless guardian.

Twice, Matt's right foot slipped out from under him, and he slid dangerously close to losing his balance on the walkway. If it hadn't been for the stout guardrail, he would have gone over the side.

Just as they got past the spraying hose, it stopped flailing and went still. A few hot, pink drops fell from the detached end.

"Well, that's just great," Justin muttered.

"Is everyone all right?" Matt asked.

"I'm all right, just soaked in oil," Catherine said.

"Me too," Stacy echoed.

"Glad that's over." Cody wiped slime from his face.

A terrible grinding sound reverberated through the complex. Sparks shot from several of the pistons, and steam erupted from somewhere below, sending a wretched cloud up at them.

One of the closest pistons seized, buckled, and started swaying back and forth.

"It's gonna fall on the walkway. Run!" Matt shouted.

"We'll be trapped on the other side," Stacy cried.

"It's where we need to be! Let's run!" Matt insisted.

Catherine and Justin raced ahead. Darin helped Stacy move as Cody and Matt brought up the rear.

The piston, even though it was one of the smaller ones, was at least three feet in diameter. Like a falling tree, it rocked in place slowly then swooped down with incredible speed.

Covered in oil, everyone slipped and slid, ending up on their knees, where they crawled over the metal grate. Through torn pants, the sharp edges of the walkway cut into their knees. Their hands fared no better, as the metal railings had become too slick to hold on to. More pistons seized and fell like timber in the forest.

The one nearest them slammed against the walkway just a few feet ahead of Catherine. She screamed as it crunched and bent the metal railings, causing the walkway to bow like a melted cassette tape left on a car's dashboard in summertime.

"What do we do?" she gasped.

"We have to keep going. It's gonna snap this walkway!" Darin shouted.

He lifted Stacy over the top of the downed piston as Justin helped Catherine and then leapt over himself. Matt jumped, but only succeeded in sliding down the greasy side. He looked to Cody and Darin, both having the same trouble as him.

"Here." Matt cupped his hands. Cody did the same. "Darin, we'll boost you."

Darin stepped up, and they heaved him over.

"Thanks," Darin shouted. "Cody, you next, and Justin and I will pull Matt over!"

Matt closed his eyes and braced for Cody's weight pulling at his sore wrist. Once Cody was firmly on the other side, Matt took a few quick steps back and ran toward the piston. He jumped, reaching for the outstretched hands hanging over the top. His wrist slipped out of one of the boys' hands, but the other grabbed Matt's shirt and found purchase. Matt desperately kicked at the side of the metal in a futile attempt to find his way over.

"I got him!" Darin yelled.

Matt slid over the top, and both Darin and Justin helped him down. He nodded in thanks—no time for anything else.

The walkway bowed beneath Matt's feet. The metal groaned under the strain, threatening to snap in an instant. "Everybody! Keep going! Hurry!"

They struggled to make the last few yards to the end of the piston forest section. Oil smoked venomously somewhere behind them.

"Almost there. Keep going!" Matt urged, as a few of them had stopped to catch their breath and look back.

"We made it," Stacy gasped.

Another piston snapped from the ceiling and fell, crashing across the other.

The walkway collapsed at the impact, and the long strip of metal leading right to where they stood came apart like a zipper.

Screams filled the air.

CHAPTER 17

The walkway toppled vertically just a few feet past Catherine, who was the farthest along the path.

Everyone managed to hold on to the railing as the causeway slipped and tumbled down. It hit something with force, sending a terrible shock like a thunderbolt back up the line.

"Guess we ain't going back that way," Justin said. He was only a few feet behind Catherine but had held on to the right side of the railing, while she was on the left.

Stacy crouched behind Catherine, Darin right behind her. Matt and Cody brought up the rear on the right side.

"I'm too greasy to climb!" Stacy wailed. She grasped the railing above her, but each time she tried to pull herself up, her fingers slipped.

"You don't have to do pull-ups on it," Darin said. "Treat it like a ladder. Nice and easy. One foot and then the other; your hands are just to keep you balanced. I won't let you fall." He spoke calmly and firmly.

"I can't," Stacy cried. "I keep slipping. I'll fall."

"I won't let you fall," Darin repeated.

His confidence gave Matt confidence. "We can do this, guys. Just take your time."

Cody reached up and grabbed ahold of the cross-section bar above him and climbed up. He made it look effortless—until he slipped.

CHAPTER 18

Matt's heart caught in his throat.

Cody's foot slid off a greasy rung, and he slipped down one section, two sections, three sections—Matt caught hold of his shirt.

"Don't you dare fall!" he shouted. Images of Kyle slipping out of his grasp and being drowned in a monster flood flashed through his mind.

"I ain't about to," Cody said as he scrambled to get back on the railing.

Matt's wrist ached. Luckily, Cody's shirt was made of a material that didn't let the hydraulic fluid make it too slippery.

Cody latched onto the railing beneath him, and Matt finally felt like he could let go.

"That was too close." Matt shook his twisted wrist.

"I hear you. Try being on the other end." Cody shook his head. "I know it ain't polite to say, but I might need to change my drawers."

"We can't afford to lose anyone," Matt declared. "Let's go slow and easy so nobody slips."

"Wipe your hands on your shirtsleeves or pants to get as much of the hydraulic fluid off as possible," Cody said.

"And let's be ready in case anyone else slips," Matt added.

Stacy whimpered. "I, like, can't do this. I'll fall just like Cody."

"I'm all right." Cody urged, "We've got to keep going."

The metal causeway groaned and moved a fraction of an inch.

Stacy screamed and clutched the railing all the tighter, her eyes clamped shut.

Darin looked at Matt. "I'm gonna need some help with her, and we gotta move."

Matt considered their options. The causeway was not wide, but he didn't dare jump from one side to the other since the grease could make him slip, not to mention a heavy jump might make the whole thing come tumbling down. Then it hit him. "I have the rope!"

"Toss it up to me, and I'll tie it off," Catherine said.

"Are you able to do that?" Cody asked.

"I'm almost to the top. Just hang on a minute," she answered.

Matt clenched his jaw, praying she wouldn't slip.

Catherine crawled her way up two more rungs to the top. She turned around on her belly and stretched her hands out to Matt. "I'm ready. Throw it to me."

He locked his legs around one of the rails and reached into the backpack with his left hand, still hooking the rail with his right. It was tricky, and he almost knocked the blueprint map out by accident, but he finally grasped the rope, took several loops in hand, and took a deep breath.

Under any other circumstances, it would have been easy to throw about twenty feet of rope ten feet up, but the slippery fluid changed everything. One wrong move could send him plummeting to his death.

Matt threw the rope too far out, and Catherine couldn't reach it.

"Stop playing around, chief," Justin said.

"Stop it. He's trying," Catherine said. "Again."

Matt looped the rope and tossed it one more time. Catherine caught it, but she didn't have a strong hold, and it fell from her grasp.

"Third time's the charm," Matt said as he looped it one last time and threw it.

Catherine caught it and edged backward out of sight. She pulled a good length of the rope from him, then called back, "I've got it as secure as I know how. I'm guessing that three big knots around an I-beam should do it."

"I'll double-check it." Justin climbed to the top and disappeared from sight for a moment before calling back, "It's good, chief!"

Matt tossed his end of the rope to Darin, who looped it around and under Stacy's arms. "You're going to have to let go of this railing and help climb. They've got you, and I'm here to be a backup."

Stacy still had her eyes shut. "I can't. I'll fall."

"No, you won't. You've got the rope, and Justin and Catherine are going to help pull you up. Just keep your hands on the railing and your feet on the rungs and help them get you up top."

"I can't." She shook her head. She still had not opened her eyes. "I'm going to totally die here!"

Matt looked at Darin, wondering what he could say to her that hadn't already been said. How could they get her to climb before it was too late? He was painfully aware of the stress on the metal and the continual light groan.

"Stacy!" Darin demanded.

Stacy cracked her eyes open to look at him. He leaned in and kissed her passionately on the mouth, and she melted into his arms.

"Now, help them get you up top, and I'll see you up there in a minute."

"Okay," she said softly. Catherine and Justin pulled on the rope, and she clambered up the railing.

Darin followed behind her, just a little bit slower, but completely free-hand in spite of the greasy surface.

Stacy crested the top. "I did it!"

The walkway shifted and dropped another couple of inches.

Darin, midstride between two railings, slipped but caught himself with one hand on the next rung down.

Stacy screamed. "Are you okay?" she called out.

Darin hung by one arm but strained and wrapped his legs around another rung. "I'm fine." He gasped for breath.

"Good thing she didn't see that," Cody whispered.

"Let's use the rope from now on," Matt said.

"Yeah." Darin nodded as he wiped beading sweat from his forehead.

We can't afford to lose anyone. Matt's own words echoed in his head.

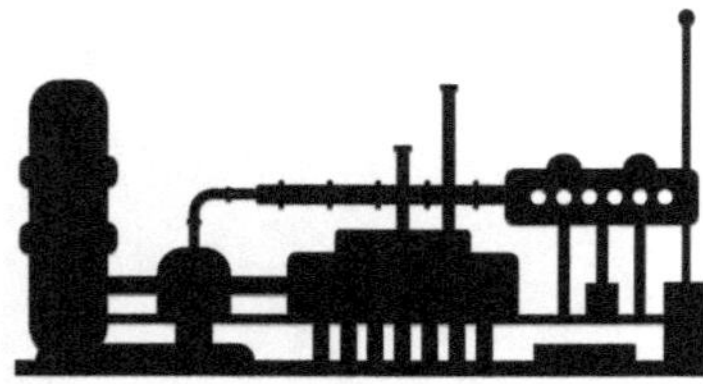

CHAPTER 19

When everyone made it to the top, they moved farther down the walkway, where they didn't have to worry about it crashing underneath them anymore, and then took a good, long breather.

"Any good way to get all of this stuff off?" Catherine asked.

"We could use gas, if we had any," Cody said.

"You mean like unleaded?"

"Yeah, it works great. But then you gotta use soap and water after that," Cody continued.

"How would you even know that?" Stacy asked.

He shrugged. "We had to do that all the time on the ranch. If we ever got tar on us, or too much bag balm, gas gets 'er right off."

"Gross," Stacy said.

Matt glanced at the blueprint map, then down the walkway. "Guys, I think that's the tram station right there!"

They hurried the final hundred yards to the station.

The tram was bigger than he had expected. Matt breathed a sigh of relief, having secretly been worried that the tram might be too small to fit all of them at the same time.

A small area jutted out right beside a suspended track. It wasn't anything elaborate, just a small bench and section where the tram was stopped. There were green and red lights on the side of the track, as if to signal when it was moving or coming to a stop. The track was a single suspended monorail. The tram hung below the track, reminding Matt of one of the rides at Disneyland. The tram itself consisted of three sections. Two pods looked like passenger cars, with plastic seats and more than enough room to carry all of them and have them stretch out, but the very back compartment was a platform. It was like the back of a flatbed truck. Attached to the platform was a robotic arm, folded up, and on the end was a big pincer. The pincer was about two feet long and looked very robust.

"Would you look at that? The robot claw!" Justin exclaimed.

"That's probably so they can load and unload construction stuff," Darin said. "Then they don't have to have a forklift for everything."

"They will when they move it," Catherine said.

"No, The Claw has the power to do all!" Justin fiddled with the control sticks at the rear of the robotic arm.

"Don't play with that. You don't know how to use it," Darin said.

"I'm just having fun is all," Justin argued as he jumped from the back of the flatcar to the walkway. "Someone has got to liven things up around here."

Stacy piped up. "Guys, the way things have been going, I don't know if we should even ride on that thing. Everything is falling apart. It's all dangerous. Let's just get out of here."

Matt looked to Darin and guessed he knew what he was thinking. As gently as he could, Matt said, "I get that, Stacy. We're all worried, and this building seems like it won't hold together very much longer, but the tram will be faster and more direct. It'll get us out of here a whole lot faster than walking."

"What if it falls?"

"Since the tram is used for hauling heavy equipment, it would be built a lot stronger than the walkways. Should be safer too," Darin said.

"So faster and safer?" she asked timidly.

"Yeah."

"Okay, let's, like, do the tram train, then." Stacy nodded, her frizzy hair bouncing a little.

Glancing at the red and green lights on the sides of the tram, Justin asked, "What do these even mean?"

"I think it's to show direction. That's my best guess," Matt said.

A shower of sparks rained down from overhead. Everyone dodged and ran for cover.

"What is with this deathtrap?!" Cody shouted.

The sparking stopped for the moment, but everyone looked about warily.

"You were saying?" Stacy said.

"All the more reason to get going out of here faster," Matt insisted.

"He's right." Darin stepped up on the flatcar. "Come on, give me your hand. Let's get moving."

Catherine and Justin followed, stepping up on the flatbed part of the tram. The whole tram swayed back and forth.

Justin again got behind the robotic arm and fiddled with the controls. "The Claw will show us the way out!" he proclaimed loudly. But as he moved a knob on the robotic arm, it elevated and swung, striking Catherine. She fell forward against the bench seats.

Justin froze, mouth open and eyes wide. Darin turned to face him, ducking to avoid getting hit by the flailing arm.

The tram hummed to life and zoomed down the track.

"Justin!" Darin yelled, trailing off into the distance.

CHAPTER 20

"Guys! Stop it!" Matt screamed, running after the departing tram. He gauged it was moving at about fifteen miles per hour.

I've gotta catch up and stop the tram! Where are Justin and Darin? Why aren't they stopping it?

Matt ran as hard as he could. He kept up with it for a moment or two, but it slowly gained more and more ground on him and continued to get farther and farther away.

Red triangle lights on the back of the tram mocked his attempt at outrunning it. The lights turned a corner and disappeared into the dark.

Matt stopped, panting hard. He put his hands on his knees. He reached out for strength inside and yelled one more time, "No!"

He couldn't remember ever having a day in his life where he had such a workout—rappelling down into the shaft, climbing up a grease-covered fallen walkway, and finally running for all he was worth after his friends in the dark. He finally heard Cody calling to him over his own panting.

"You all, right?" Cody asked.

"Yeah, I couldn't catch them."

"I can see that. We gotta go back for Stacy. She can't move nearly as fast as us."

"Is she okay?"

"She ain't freaking out, if that's what you mean." Cody put a hand on Matt's shoulder and helped him up.

"They're gone," Matt said.

"I hope Catherine is all right." Cody shook his head. "But Darin and Justin will figure something out. It's got to stop sometime. We'll find 'em."

"You're right," Matt agreed. "They'll have the common sense to get off at the mountain."

"Yep," Cody said.

Matt looked at his feet, his shoulders slumped. He had tried so hard to hold them together and get through this way. He had been sure this would be safer than above ground, but now the group was torn in half. And he was scared.

"I know what you're thinking, and it's not your fault," Cody said. "Don't beat yourself up about it."

"I should have been in the pilot's seat for that thing. I should have stopped Justin from playing with that arm."

"Coulda, shoulda, woulda," Cody said. "Let's go get Stacy and get after them. We'll find them."

Matt nodded. "Thanks."

Stacy was hobbling down the track after them. "Not all of us can run, you guys."

"I'm sorry," Matt said. "I thought I could catch them and figure out how to stop it."

"I'm glad you didn't catch them. I'd rather it be three of us together than just two," she said. "If Darin can figure out how to stop it, he will."

"You're right. Let's keep following this track. We'll catch up to them soon enough, and we're still all heading toward the mountain," Matt said.

"Could you see them when you ran after them?" Stacy asked.

"I couldn't. They were all low on the floor. Catherine got hit in the head. Maybe Justin and Darin did too?" Cody said.

"We'll find our friends. It'll be okay." Matt's words were as much to convince himself as the others.

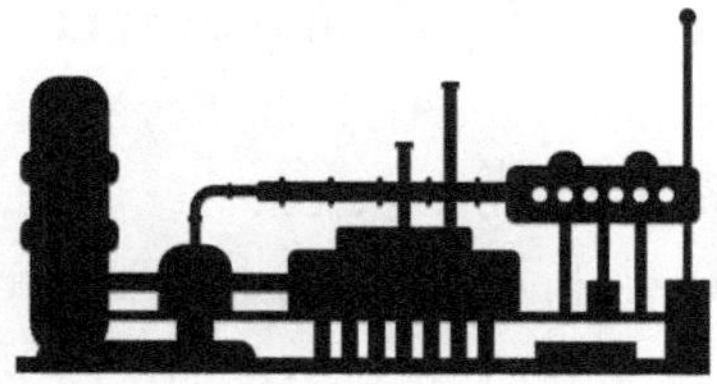

CHAPTER 21

"We better get moving if we're going to find them," Cody said.

"Do you think they're all right?" Stacy asked.

"Are *you* all right?" Matt put an arm around her.

"I think so. I mean, yes, I am. I just want to find them and get everyone back together—it's just . . . I'm holding you up."

"It's not your fault." Matt thought back to when Kim nearly got them all killed in the forest by refusing to walk. "It could have been any one of us that got hurt. We're not going to leave you behind."

"Guys." Cody spun about, already walking in the direction of the vanished tram.

"We're coming." Matt stayed close to Stacy, making sure she was walking as well as she could on her own. He was glad she was stepping up and not having any problems with Darin's being hit and speeding off on the tram. He squelched a bit of anger at Justin for messing with the robotic arm. He knew it hadn't been on purpose. Who could have known what this place would do? It was all falling apart. It seemed to be shaking itself to pieces from the very force of the crazy natural calamities it was trying to inflict on them topside. At least they were inside it now, where they were better protected.

Along the way, there were spots where the metal paneling was rusting and even starting to bend under stress fractures. Here and there, wires as big as Matt's thigh sparked as the lines were pushed and ripped out by the building falling apart. There were places where natural roots had grown and forced seams in the metal to snap.

"That looks just like where I've seen weeds growing in asphalt," Stacy said.

"Yeah, and even without the benefit of sunlight down here," Cody added.

"I guess even these flickering lights do enough to give them some kind of photosynthesis," Matt said.

Brighter light met them as they rounded a big bend on the tram and causeway. Another vent, open to the sky, allowed light to filter down from above, but this seemed a little different than the one they had first come down.

"Is it open all the way?" Stacy asked.

"I'm guessing it's a vent of some kind, like the one we came down before, but I think it's even bigger," Cody said.

"Almost, but it's vertical. There's no way up. Not that it matters. Our friends are still on the tram and went past this a long time ago," Matt said, taking a look up the shaft. "There used to be some flow vents, but they look broken, like they got blasted out."

"What?" Cody looked closer at the long scratch

marks showing where terrific forces had pushed the vents out and scratched deep grooves into the metal siding.

"A vent for what?" Stacy asked.

"Maybe where the storms came from," Matt offered.

"I don't like the sound of that."

"You're gonna like this even less," Cody said.

Massive fans with blades as long as semitruck trailers came into view. There were six blades on each motor mount, pointing toward the shaft.

"So this thing makes tornados?" Stacy asked.

"It looks that way. They look kinda like the ones we saw in the junkyard," Cody said.

"Good thing they aren't on. We'd be blown away."

"Literally," Cody said warily.

"The air feels colder here, even though we just saw a little sunlight," Stacy noted.

"You're right, and it's not just the shadow," Matt said.

Cody shook his head. "I don't want to agree with y'all, but I'm gonna have to. This is downright chilly for my Texas blood."

Just past the giant fans, the air grew colder still, their breath puffing white clouds in front of them as they exhaled.

"We're at another door," Cody said. "It has frost on it."

"A freezer?" Stacy asked.

"Looks like. Awful big too." Cody tapped on it.

Matt frowned. "Our friends rode the tram through here, so we've gotta follow." He pushed the button, and the doors opened with a sci-fi-esque *swish*. A blast of even colder air hit them. The doors remained open, letting the cold out into the warmer chamber. On the far side of the walkway stood another open door.

"Whoa!" Cody gripped his shoulders at the cold.

Matt stepped forward to look inside, and the others followed.

Inside the freezer complex, lights covered with little black cages gave off just enough illumination for them to see that it was like a giant rectangular box lined with a multitude of pipes and what looked like fire extinguisher sprinklers.

"This is for making snow." Stacy smiled, then shrugged. "I told you I used to ski."

The walkway widened out inside the freezer to about thirty feet, then narrowed on the other side back to its normal width.

"This is weird," Cody said.

"Yeah, but at least it shows that it was made for people to be in here to do maintenance and whatnot, and we can keep going to follow the tram."

"I don't see the tram tracks in here," Cody said. "It must have gone around the backside of this freezer."

"Do we have to go in there?" Stacy asked.

"I don't see any other way." Matt replied.

He took a step forward and the walkway swayed. The large freezer had no bottom to it. The ice-covered grating gave Matt vertigo as he stared into the foggy abyss below.

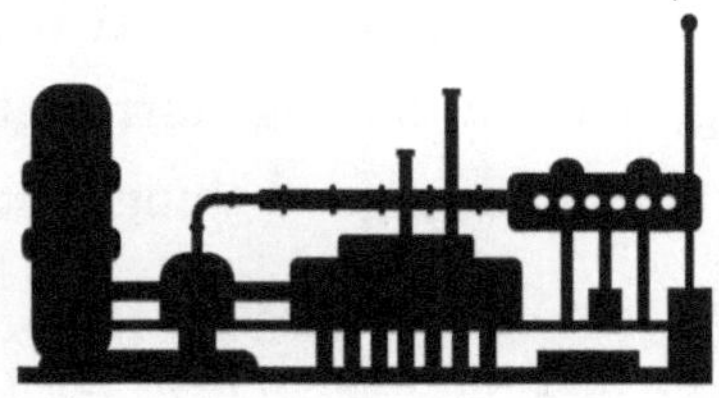

CHAPTER 22

Each step they took on the walkway caused chunks of ice to fall into the darkness below them. The box continued downward as far as they could see, all lined with the pipes and spigots. Extra pipes like the ones lining the walls lay on the walkway, along with a box of tools.

"Look at the size of this thing, all just to make it snow like crazy outside," Matt said. The ingenuity to create the fake climate outside was beyond the scope of anything he had ever seen before.

Cody, however, was more interested in the tools at their feet. "Can't believe they just left this stuff lying here."

"I guess they just didn't care enough to haul them out," Stacy said.

"Well, they should have. The cold can't be good for them," Cody explained.

"Maybe they knew they would need to get to them in a hurry to do repairs," Matt offered.

Cody shook his head. "They should have left them out of the cold. It will make them break easier."

"Speaking of 'break easier,' let's get out of here. My nose is freezing, and my hair is starting to get frosted highlights, and that's not a good thing," Stacy said with a laugh.

Ice crystals formed on Matt's nose from the sub-zero temperature. Everything in sight had a thick layer of frost. It was the biggest freezer he had ever seen. "All right, let's go." He crossed the stack of pipes and headed toward the open door on the far side of the box.

A tremor rocked the freezer, and the cold metal of the walkway twisted like a giant was playing jump rope.

They all held on to the railing, and just as soon as it had begun, it was over. The frigid cold metal inflamed their palms.

"What was that?" Stacy cried.

"This whole place is breaking down," Matt said. "Let's move!"

The doors behind them whisked shut with the tremor. They could just barely hear the *swish* of them shutting. The warmer temperature from the open chamber dissipated, and the room grew colder. The doors in front of them began to close too.

"Run!" Matt shouted, slipping on the frozen catwalk.

Cody raced ahead to catch the door while Stacy hobbled as fast as she could, but none of them were fast enough. The doors shut.

Cody pressed the round door-release button, but nothing happened. "It's not working!"

Stacy screamed as she reached the door. "This is too cold!"

"I'll go try the one we came in." Cody hurried back the other way.

Matt continued pressing the button to see if it might work after one, two, ten more tries. He jiggled the latch, but it wouldn't budge.

Cody returned. "I tried it like twenty times. It's not working. Like the quake broke it or made it lock or something."

"We're trapped." Matt slammed his fist against the door.

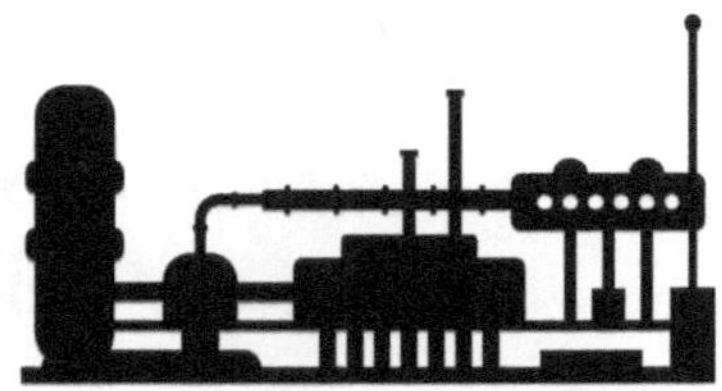

CHAPTER 23

"Get us out of here!" Stacy screamed.

"You've got to calm down. We'll figure this out," Matt said. They weren't dressed for this kind of cold. He knew they had to figure something out fast.

Looking over their heads, Matt realized he had missed something. There was a massive fan above them. Once it turned on and the spigots released water, this room would fill with snow that the fan would blast out and away. The blizzard. It had originated here. The avalanche. Nathan . . . He shook his head. He had to focus. He could only imagine how cold that fan would make things. As it was, he was afraid they wouldn't be able to last more than an hour in these temps.

Cody and Matt spoke at the same time. "The tools!"

Stacy crouched down on her heels and shivered while Matt and Cody raced to grab the tools from the middle of the walkway.

They pulled their shirtsleeves over their hands to hold the frozen tools—a big pipe wrench and a set of iron clamps. Racing back, they pounded on the door. But the thick steel held off their attempts like a backboard versus a basketball.

"We're not doing anything," Cody said.

"The latch," Matt suggested.

They took turns hitting the latch, oblivious to Stacy screaming at them to stop.

The latch snapped off and struck the walkway. It landed with a cold, cruel clank, knocking off another hint of frost that fell away into the darkness.

"I told you! But you lunkheads wouldn't listen!" Stacy shouted. "This is all your fault. We shouldn't have come in here, and you shouldn't have let the door shut! And now we're all gonna die!"

"She ain't wrong," Cody said. "We gotta get out of here quick, or we'll be Popsicles."

CHAPTER 24

Battering the door hadn't gotten them anywhere. Matt scanned what they had on hand and tried to think of a way to get out.

Monkey wrenches, iron clamps, big pipe wrenches, and all of the extra pipes lay on the walkway. He looked up at the fan and then at the caged lights.

Stacy had started to sob.

Cody put a hand on her shoulder. "Those tears will freeze on your face. You don't want that, do you?"

"It doesn't matter. We're gonna die in here," she said.

"No, we're not," Matt declared. "Cody, help me with one of those pipes and clamps. I've got an idea."

Matt stood on one of the railings of the walkway and stretched to reach one of the cage lights. He gauged how hard to hit and knocked one of the cages off from around the bulb without damaging the light.

Cody shivered. "I think I got an idea of what you're doing." He handed one of the clamps to Matt, then one of the pipes. It took two pipes to reach the door, but they spun them together and slammed it right up against the seam where the door opened.

"Hand me some ice," Matt said.

Cody used a wrench to break off a big chunk next to the door. He handed the piece to Matt, who held it up against the bulb. Water slowly trickled from his hand and ran through the pipe toward the door.

"Hold it right up against where the latch was. If the water freezes and expands there, maybe it will pop it open," Matt said.

It was slow, cold going. Matt's hands turned red and sore. Then before long, he couldn't even feel his hands from the cold of holding ice and cold water.

The water froze in the pipe, but enough of it kept running down that, slowly but surely, the lock and broken latch started expanding inside.

Matt's hands throbbed. The bulb burst, and a small section of the freezer dimmed.

"Now what?" Stacy asked.

"We keep trying with another bulb," Matt answered.

They moved the pipes to another bulb at the opposite side of the walkway and started over. Matt's sleeves, covered in ice, crunched with his movements. He knew hypothermia was setting in because he no longer shivered, but if he didn't keep going, they would all freeze to death. Matt closed his eyes, remembering his mom. Focusing all his efforts for just a mere second put him in a state his mom called Matt-itation. He instantly felt his heart rate slow, and the corners of his mouth tugged into a slight smile. Suddenly, he had the confidence that this part of the puzzle would be solved.

They watched intently as water slowly entered the crack in the door, and the freezing water forced it open a micron at a time.

It was now open almost a half-inch.

"It's a difference, but I don't know if that's enough to do anything." Cody's face was red and looked chapped.

Matt guessed his own must look the same. "We've got to keep trying."

A loud crack came from the door as they melted one more chunk into the broken latch. The expanding ice snapped and popped as it refroze. Another pop was followed by metal snapping.

Stacy took a monkey wrench and pounded on the door. "Open!" she cried, then dropped down, exasperated.

Another crack and pop of ice, and the door shifted, opening a bare two inches that seemed like a mile to the frozen teens.

Cody put the wrench into the gap and pried with all his strength. Matt slammed a pipe into the gap and joined in. The door gave up and slid open. The air outside the freezer felt like a tropical breeze compared to the icy hell they'd endured.

They said nothing as they took a long moment away from the freezer to warm up.

"I don't think I ever want to eat ice cream again," Stacy whispered.

"I don't ever want to leave Texas again," Cody said.

"Or Nevada." Matt blew into his hands to warm them up faster.

"I think I want to move somewhere even warmer than those places," Stacy said. "Maybe the sun."

After the feeling slunk painfully back into his hands, Matt said, "We gotta keep moving. They've got a huge lead on us."

Cody gave a brief sigh but stood up. He still looked awfully red, and Matt guessed the cold had been pretty hard on him.

"We'll take it easy, but we gotta get the blood flowing in our limbs."

"You're right," Cody agreed. "I don't think I've ever been this tired. Not even after a day of branding."

They made their way along the walkway. The tram tracks looped around the freezer and disappeared behind a massive pillar of rock. As they went around the big obstacle, they saw another building.

CHAPTER 25

The building hung beside the suspended tram track and walkway. A new track held big, bowl-like containers along the opposite side, hanging from the suspension system like enormous pots ready for a giant cook.

"What the heck are those, guys?" Stacy asked.

"I don't know." Matt shook his head.

"I bet Darin would know," she said quietly.

"They look almost like some of the big industrial vats I've seen that pour molten iron in the factory down the road from my old house," Cody answered.

As they got closer, they could see that the vats were full of a dark brown, sludge-type material.

"At least the air is warmer here," Cody offered.

"Yeah, but it smells like crap." Stacy made a gag-me sign. "Actual crap."

"At least we aren't freezing," Matt said.

Cody laughed. "That, little lady, is the smell of chemical fertilizer. Maybe that's what these vats do, fertilize all the trees and growing things in the whole complex."

"Gross." She pinched her nose.

As they got closer to the building, Matt pointed to a number fifteen on the door. He looked all around them, determined to be more cautious this time, and inspected the suspension area of what he assumed to be the control building for the vats of fertilizer. He didn't see any rust on the cables or anything else that looked like it might fall apart like some of the places they went past earlier.

"It looks safe enough." He patted the side of the trailer.

"That's what you said about the freezer," Stacy said.

"I don't think I said that."

"It looks okay to me too," Cody agreed. "Let's see if there's anything inside to help us figure out where we are."

They opened the standard door and went inside. This office was a little bit different from the earlier job-type trailer. There were botany illustrations on the wall and a small lab section with Erlenmeyer flasks and beakers with some dried chemical substances. There were bags of fertilizer in the corner. One of them was open and spilled out onto the floor. Everything was covered in dust.

"What's with the fertilizer? It's not like even those fifty-pound bags are enough to fill one of the vats," Stacy said.

"Probably just them working on formulas or somethin'," Cody said.

"Whoever it was, it looks like they left in a hurry. They couldn't even clean up the mess," Matt observed.

"The door said this is building fifteen. Let's look at your map and get our bearings straight," Cody suggested.

Matt pulled out the blueprints and spread them on the desk. "We're here." He pointed to the number fifteen on the blueprints. "Sub-level fifteen, fertilizer section."

"Kinda funny they kept the freezer next to the plant food," Stacy said.

"I don't understand any of the logic of this place." Cody wrinkled his brow. "Don't make a bit of sense."

"There's the mountain," Matt said. "But at this point, I think we need to put that on the backburner until we find the others."

"Agreed." Cody nodded.

"Definitely," Stacy chimed in.

Matt looked up at her. "You feeling better?"

"I'm always doing better when I'm not freezing to death," she said.

Matt shook his head. "So we're agreed. We find our friends, then worry about the mountain. Looks like the tram went around this bend and there's another stopping point here, so if we're lucky, maybe the tram came to a stop, and they were able to get off?"

"Let's go see," Cody said. "At least the tram track and our walkway stay together for a good long ways, instead of like that freezer split."

"Yeah." Matt's hands still hurt from holding the ice up to the light bulbs. *I hope I don't have frostbite.*

They left the building. The smell of fertilizer was so strong, Matt felt like it was permeating his clothes.

"Ugh, that smell," Stacy complained.

"At least it's warm," Cody joked.

"Yeah, but this?" She shook her head. "I need a shower just smelling it."

"That's why it's stronger now." Matt pointed at the vats under the walkway. They hung under a suspension track that could move whichever way the fertilizer line needed to send them, all over the complex. Matt peeked over an edge and screwed up his face at the brown slurry resembling gallons of raw sewage.

"Did you see that?" he asked.

"Looks like the bottom of an outhouse," Cody said.

Stacy held her nose. "Don't remind me. I had to use one at the county fair once. Second worst night of my life."

"And the first?"

"When I woke up here," she said.

CHAPTER 26

The automation line suddenly hummed into a moving frenzy. Every single vat gave a loud clack as it moved down the conveyor belt, bumping along the suspension bridge. The sloppy sound of more fertilizer being dumped into the empty vats made Matt and Cody giggle.

"Boys and their potty humor. Lance-Darin wouldn't laugh at that. He's mature." Stacy groaned. "Let's get out of here."

"Hang on, let's see what it does before we just leave," Matt said.

"Why, so you can both make more fart jokes?"

"We never made any fart jokes." Cody chuckled.

Stacy rolled her eyes. Matt and Cody stifled laughter as the vats were filled, then moved down the line toward bulbs where tree roots dangled. The clear bulbs had hinges that opened wide, exposing the roots of the trees hanging down into the void. The moving vats, which were over eight feet wide in diameter and ten feet tall, hung on a special track, elevated by a chain system. Once in place, the roots were coated with the goopy fertilizer slurry. Within just a few seconds, the clear bulb would close over the roots again and fill with water from an automation system hidden somewhere inside the ceiling. They watched as the water and fertilizer mixed together.

"It's efficient," Matt said.

"I guess. Don't know why you couldn't just do it topside, though," Cody said. "I guarantee that would be cheaper."

"Not if you're worried about getting killed by volcanoes and blizzards," Stacy retorted.

"She's got a point," Matt said.

"I guess." Cody scratched his neck. "But I was just thinking about all of this and how much work it must be to mechanize every little thing, even caring for trees and fake lakes, and now no one is down here making sure the machines run smoothly. Everything has to be greased and managed, or it breaks down."

Matt stared at something in the distance. He stepped away from the others, much to their confusion.

"Matt? What did I say?" Cody asked.

Matt turned with a grin. "You said that the machines break down, and look at that!" He pointed down the track toward a tram car with their friends aboard. They could just make out Justin, Darin, and Catherine standing on the flatcar.

They rushed down the causeway, hooting and hollering in glee. "Darin! Catherine! Justin! Down here!"

They called back and waved, but Matt couldn't make out the words amidst the noise of the fertilizer vats and the groaning chains of the feeding system.

The causeway stretched way out, revealing a large, open space, wider than a football stadium, the boundaries lost in the darkness. Taking stock of the peculiar open area, Matt noticed massive fans in the ceiling. What could they be for? A wind tunnel in a basement? "Do you see that, Cody?"

"Yeah, must be a place where they make the non-frozen windstorms and tornados. The people that dreamt this stuff up are real creeps."

"Hold on, guys! I can't run as fast as you, remember?" Stacy called.

They slowed to wait for her despite being anxious to talk to their friends again. "Why do you think they stopped out in this wide-open space?" Cody asked.

"Maybe they finally figured out how to stop it, and it's just good luck that it was kinda close by." Matt shrugged.

A sprinkle of dirt hit Matt's shoulder, and he moved forward, dodging the falling particles. One of the plastic bulb covers opened, jammed with roots dangling outward. The fertilizer vat spread its goo, but as it started to move on, it struck the bulb, breaking it. The water mixture sprayed, but without the plastic bulb to hold the slurry, the earth and water fell to the causeway below in a muddy heap. The dirt around the tree was washed away by the automatic watering cables, and the tree slipped. Matt stared in horror as the tree slammed into the walkway with a great crash—separating him, Cody, and Stacy.

Matt raced ahead, while Stacy and Cody jumped back toward the fertilizer building.

The causeway groaned under the strain of the enormous tree, and metal girders snapped with loud pings.

Matt slid as the causeway tore away from its supports. His friends on the tram screamed, but they could do nothing to stop the terrible tug of gravity.

Matt grabbed the edge of the railing as the causeway bent nearly vertical.

Straining to hold on, he glanced up at Stacy and Cody. "Oh no!" he cried. "Guys!"

Cody and Stacy fell into one of the vats covered in the fertilizer slurry as it jerked along on the chain-driven link to feed the artificial forest.

Darin, Catherine, and Justin shouted Matt's name. He could barely make it out above the din of the machinery.

The causeway bent and rumbled, spurring Matt to act before the entire section fell with the tree into the dark abyss below.

The vat containing the goo-covered Cody and Stacy bumped along below him and farther back along the way they'd come.

"Matt! Drop into the next vat!" Darin called.

What? That was crazy. Then he would be as stuck as Cody and Stacy.

"The walkway is collapsing!" Justin shouted. "Hurry!"

"The vat will go right under us!" Catherine cried. "We've got you. Just jump in!"

Understanding dawned, and with a groan, Matt dropped into the horrid-looking brown mass. It felt like a massive, thick mud pie. He was grateful that it only went to his knees and not over his head. With some difficulty, he could almost get a leg out, but the other stuck farther down. This was gonna be tricky.

The walls of the vat were high enough that Matt couldn't see much of anything except those ominous fans in the ceiling and more sunlight now. Why was that? Oh yeah, there was a big, exposed hole from where the tree fell inside. *Built to last*, he mused.

"Matt, we're right behind you," Cody called. "Looks like we'll get to the tram, just a little dirty for wear."

"This is so gross!" Stacy shouted.

CHAPTER 27

"Matt, are you okay?" Catherine called.

"Never better. Oh wait, except that I'm stuck up to my knees in this muck!" he shouted back.

"At least it's not in your hair," Stacy answered from the next vat over. "I fell in, and Cody landed on top of me!"

"Not my fault when trees are falling from the sky." Cody laughed.

"We'll get you out with the robot arm," Darin shouted. "I think I've got the hang of it."

"I sure hope so," Matt said. "I don't want to get pressed into tree fertilizer."

The fertilizer vat line ran just a few feet beneath the tram track. Matt knew he couldn't reach the tram line on his own unless maybe he was able to climb on top of the vat, but he was stuck in the fertilizer goo like a rat in a cage.

"So long as the tram battery is on, we're good," Darin

answered. "I'm gonna reach down to get you as soon as you get here. Should be in about one minute."

"What about us?" Stacy cried.

"I'll get you too," Darin said firmly. "We can time it right so long as everyone keeps cool. Can you keep cool?"

"I can keep cool," Stacy whimpered.

"It's all right," Cody said. "I'm here to help you."

"Oh crap," Justin said.

"What's 'oh crap'?" Matt called.

"Justin bumped against the ignition switch, and it broke off. We'll get it," Darin answered.

"I don't want to die," Stacy whined.

"You're not gonna die," Darin shouted. "I'll get you."

The clanking of the vats on the chain drive kept a malevolent beat like one of those German industrial bands. Matt did his best to extricate himself from the morass of sticky fertilizer, but it was hard going. Again, he thought that if he could climb to the rim of the vat, he wouldn't be dependent on the robotic arm. But climbing was not as easy as thinking about it.

"I think I can hot-wire it," Justin said.

"Hurry!" Catherine said.

"I'm trying," he grunted.

"Coming up quick, Matt. Be ready," Darin called.

"Is the arm working?" Matt asked.

"Not yet, but I'll pull you up if I have to hang upside down like a monkey."

"No, Lance-Darin, don't risk it. Save yourself!" Stacy shouted.

"It's gonna be okay. Almost here," Darin shouted. "Get ready, Matt!"

The vat banged along the track, keeping a rock-steady beat as the chain thumped like a drum machine.

Matt finally caught a glimpse of the tram and Darin leaning far over the edge, ready to lunge and grab him. The look of frustration on his sweaty face made it clear that the distance was farther than he had hoped.

"Got it!" Justin shouted as the tram engine crackled to life.

Darin manipulated the arm down into the vat. Matt grabbed hold, and the arm lifted him out of the muck and up onto the flatbed of the tram just before the vat, continuing its rhythmic beat down the track, traveled out of reach.

"We're gonna have to be really quick to get two people out. I barely made it with Matt," Darin alerted Cody and Stacy as the vat they were in neared the tram.

"I've got my rope. You get Stacy with the arm, and Cody, grab the rope!" Matt shouted.

"I'll be ready," Cody answered.

Matt unwound the rope and tossed it into the vat before Darin could even maneuver the arm down.

Cody helped Stacy climb onto the robot arm and only then took hold of the rope. Darin lifted Stacy to safety just before the vat ducked under the tram track.

Matt moved along the side of the tram flatcar. "Cody, I've got you. Let's pull you out." He heaved backward with Catherine and Justin's help.

"I'm having a hard time holding on. I'm slick with this slime," Cody said. "It got all over my hands and clothes."

"Wrap it around yourself," Matt answered.

"I'll try, but I'm running out of rope while this thing is moving," Cody said.

"Pull!" Matt shouted.

They pulled and pulled, and Cody came up out of the vat but dangled alongside the big bowl. He gradually slid back down the rope, only holding onto it with his goo-covered hands.

"Can you move the arm over there?" Matt asked.

"It won't reach that far," Darin answered.

"Come on, Cody, hang on till I can reach you," Matt grunted. "Guys take the rope; I'll reach for him."

Darin took Matt's place pulling the rope, while Matt bent down at the edge of the tram to reach for Cody's hand.

Cody slipped farther down the rope. Each tug only seemed to steal more line from his grasp.

Matt watched in horror as he strained to reach his friend. Visions of Kyle slipping away flashed, haunting him. This time, it wasn't turbulent waters that would carry his friend away, but the all-encompassing darkness below.

"I'm slipping." Cody's eyes widened.

Matt stretched as far as he could, but Cody's hand was still inches away, then farther as he slipped again, as if in slow motion.

Cody reached the end of the rope—and plunged into oblivion.

"No!" Matt screamed as Cody disappeared into shadow.

"What? No!" Catherine cried. "No! He didn't fall. He *couldn't*!"

Justin took her in his arms.

"Is he . . . dead?" Stacy asked.

Darin nodded, and she buried her face into his chest.

Matt remained prostrate on the flatcar, staring into darkness. "I failed again," he muttered as he pushed himself to his knees. He stared straight ahead at nothing, fists clenched at his sides and teeth clamped together, willing himself not to lose it as pressure built up in his eyes.

A terrific crash brought daylight streaming down a few yards away. Another tree fell in a shower of dirt and debris as yet another mechanical mishap caused the ceiling and fertilizer units to break down.

"If you can get the tram running, get us out of here," Matt ordered.

"What about Cody?" Justin argued.

"He's gone, and if we don't get moving, we'll be joining him. Get us out of here."

Fifty yards away, another bulb and tree broke through, and a huge piece of the ceiling fell, ripping a massive gash in the artificial world above. This brought in a burst of light, changing what had been perpetual twilight below into midday.

A beam of light revealed a large reservoir beneath them. The banging of the metal fertilizer vats and chain drive had hidden the sound of the trees and dirt splashing into the gigantic lake below.

They all glanced down and shouted in joy.

Cody was alive and treading water.

CHAPTER 28

The boundaries of the enormous reservoir stretched farther into the shadows than they could see.

"Is there anything we can throw him?" Justin asked. "Like a life preserver?"

"There's nothing like that on the tram," Darin answered.

"He could swim to a tree to float," Stacy offered.

"Can your rope reach him?" Catherine asked. "Maybe now he won't be as slippery."

"Yeah, he's had a bath the hard way!" Justin said with a nervous laugh.

"Cody! Can you hear us?" Matt called.

Cody swam toward a tree far below.

Another crash behind them rocked the tram's rail as a falling section of the ceiling slammed against it. Brighter sunlight revealed more of the reservoir and beyond.

"Matt was right. If we don't move, we're all going down with Cody," Darin shouted.

"Let's move and figure out how to help him when we're away from this crashing," Catherine agreed.

Justin stepped to the controls and started the tram gliding along. As they moved and more light shined down, an empty concrete canal and spillway revealed itself. Because of the direction of the sunlight, the back of the reservoir was still hard to see. The light didn't reach that far. The large fans slowly turned above them. More sections of the roof and forest collapsed around them.

"Go faster!" Stacy shouted.

"I can only do so much; it won't let me go any faster!" Justin yelled back.

"Hurry!" Catherine cried.

A bulb burst beside them, showering plastic and dirt down on them and the tram track, causing the tram to bump hard and almost derail. It moved another thirty feet and came to a screeching halt.

"Did we hit something?" Stacy asked.

"No." Justin glanced over the controls. "We lost power."

"Get us moving!" Darin barked.

Another chunk of the ceiling fell just a few yards away to their right.

Catherine looked down. "I can't see Cody anymore. I hope he didn't get hit with something."

"He's there." Matt pointed back to where he could see his friend dog-paddling amidst the dirty, swollen reservoir.

"The tram car can't go anywhere. It's stopped because of sporadic power surges. But there's an onboard battery that charged when the tram was running," Justin said.

"Can you get it going again?" Darin asked.

"For a fourth time now? Yeah, I think so."

Justin pulled out wires from a speaker system. He thumbed through the different wires and terminals underneath the control panel. Matt anxiously watched him while keeping an eye on Cody. Justin took a pair of long red and black wires from the speakers and connected them to the spare battery. Sparks jumped from exposed wires.

"Be careful," Catherine cautioned.

"Trust me," Justin said with a smirk.

More of the roof caved in a short distance away, but for the moment, their position was untouched.

Matt watched Cody swimming along. "He's getting closer. My rope could probably reach him now."

"I've got an idea as soon as someone gets the power back on," Darin said.

"Working on it!" Justin hollered in response.

"Throw your rope to Cody and tell him to make a seat. If this gets some power, I think we won't need to muscle him all the way up," Darin explained.

Matt nodded in appreciation and shouted, "Cody! I'm gonna toss you the rope. Make a seat, and we'll get you up!" He couldn't hear Cody's response, but he could see a big thumbs-up. Matt couldn't believe Cody had survived that horrific fall, but he was so thankful. He tossed the rope down. It took most of the length to reach all the way down to the reservoir. Cody must have fallen almost a hundred feet. It was incredible, but the Texan was sure tough.

Darin took the end of the rope and attached it firmly to the robotic arm's pincer.

"What's that gonna do?" Stacy asked. "It can't lift him all the way up here."

"Just wait," Darin said. "This arm has got some neat tricks. Do you have power yet?"

"Almost," Justin answered as another big shower of sparks shot from the control panel. "Got it!"

"Is Cody to the rope yet?" Darin asked.

"Yeah, he gave me another thumbs-up. He must have made a seat for himself," Matt answered.

"Watch this." Darin flipped a switch on the robotic arm's control panel. The pincer spun incredibly fast, looping the rope around itself, and brought Cody zooming up. "Just let me know when he gets close so I can slow it down. Don't want him slamming his head against the rail."

"Bitchin'!" Stacy yelled. "I totally knew you'd save us, Lance-Darin!"

"I'm watching," Matt said, ignoring her.

Cody zipped up into the air as the robotic arm grew fatter and fatter with the looped rope.

"Slow it down. He's almost here," Matt said.

Darin slowed the spinning pincer.

"Okay, stop," Matt said.

Darin stopped the arm as Matt sighed. "We've got him." He helped Cody climb over the side.

Cody breathed hard as water dripped from his hair and clothes. "Talk about one heckuva swimmin' lesson. I never want to do that again."

Catherine hugged him, and then Cody tromped into

the nearest covered tram car and collapsed onto one of the sofas.

Justin was finishing his rewiring job when Matt noticed a screen with a small menu and a list of numbers. They corresponded to those on the blueprint map and to different tram stations. Some of the stations were near maintenance buildings, and other stations were just junctions. The screen itself was black, and the writing on the menu was in green DOS-style text. Matt looked at the blueprints and the next stations, and in his mind, he used these station markers as breadcrumb-style points on a map.

"The next station is twenty-three. But if we skip it, we can go right to the mountain, thirty-six," Matt said.

"How do we do that?" Catherine asked.

"Right here, it shows a way to program it where you want to go, but you can't really type on this, so I'm not sure how to bypass the other stops."

Catherine smiled. "It's simple. I guess you never took accounting?"

"No, I didn't."

"Use the down arrow and scroll to thirty-six." She moved the cursor and hit the enter button. The tram took off with just a few more bumps from debris on the tracks.

"Good work, brainiac!" Stacy said. "You must have been in one of those AP groups."

"Thanks." Catherine blushed.

Justin smiled at her. "Maybe you want to help me drive?"

"Sure." Catherine sat beside him in the front seat of

the first car. The crimson shade her face had turned deepened.

Matt's stomach churned with a touch of jealousy as he watched them.

Stacy lounged on the back seat of the first car while Matt and Cody spread out on the middle passenger car's front seat. Darin remained on the flatcar, working the robot arm, carefully unwinding the rope into a neat coil on the floor.

The tram zoomed forward for another few hundred yards, then slowed to a stop.

"Out of power again. Are you kidding me?" Darin shouted.

"Maybe you used all the juice with your rope trick," Justin shot back.

"That's not fair. We had to get Cody," Catherine said.

"I'm grateful y'all got me out of the drink, but can we get moving again?" Cody said.

Sparks blasted Justin in the face. "Ouch!" He jerked back and rubbed his eyes. "Those suckers have a lot of power."

"Did you fry the whole system?" Stacy asked.

"I dunno." Justin returned to getting the tram going.

CHAPTER 29

Justin messed with the power and disconnected the wires, wiping the ends down on his shirt then reconnecting them again. The tram moved forward ten feet. "Yes!" Justin shouted.

The tram stopped again. "No!"

He repeated the process and was able to make it go again, but each time it only seemed to have enough power to move the same ten feet, jarring everyone each time it came to a stop.

"Do you need help?" Darin asked as he finished spooling the rope and lugged it back over to Matt.

"I got it. There must be a short in the line," Justin answered angrily.

"Just get it figured out!"

"I will," he muttered. "I think I liked your leadership approach better, chief."

Matt shrugged and stuffed the rope into his pack.

The vats on the chain system continued lifting their payloads of slurry beside the stuck tram, doing their programmed feeding routine despite the ceiling caving in around them.

Matt noticed a missing section of roof that the vats were approaching. "That won't end well," he said, pointing it out to Cody.

The line of vats continued on until they had almost reached the broken section of ceiling. A great rip and popping sounded, like buttons on a fat man's shirt snapping, as the support bolts for the chain drive fell and the vats began dropping. This made the ceiling break apart more.

Almost a full football field away, a few trees in the forest above began to bend and sway, then fell into the reservoir below. It was like the forest was all jumping in for a swim. Vats continued to lift as the column moved along, but the strain was too much for the failing ceiling. Trees and plastic bulbs crashed down, hitting a massive spinning fan. The huge fan blade, as long as a tractor trailer, snapped and plunged onto the track like a knife, slicing the track cleanly in half. The tram shook like an earthquake. It swung to and fro, reminding Matt of trying to balance on top of a barbed-wire fence. Without the stability of a solid track, the high-strung tramline was just a long piece of metal waving in the wind.

"Everybody, hold on!" Darin cried.

"I think I got the power back!" Justin said excitedly.

"You missed it," Catherine said. "We can't go forward anymore."

"Why not?" he asked, incredulous.

"It's gone. The track's gone."

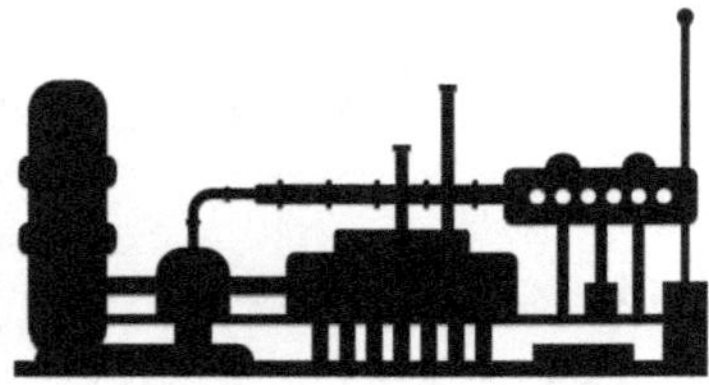

CHAPTER 30

Everything was caving in. Dirt, trees, bushes, rocks, fans, metal, and grates showered down, covering them in their weak shelter inside the tram cars. The beating on the roof sounded like *The Gong Show* gone wild, while a multitude of dents magically appeared in the ceiling. The suspended track swayed, wobbled, and began to tip lower.

"I got a bad feeling about this," Justin murmured.

"I don't like this!" Stacy shrieked.

They were all thrown forward, as if heading down a very steep hill.

Stacy and Catherine screamed. Justin swore. Matt realized he was screaming too, but Cody, who had so recently taken a high dive, remained silent.

"Everyone, hold on!" Darin shouted again.

The tram slid toward the end of the line, which dipped sharply down into the dark waters of the reservoir.

Darin swung the robot pincer arm around to grab hold of the track above and behind them, bringing their descent to an abrupt stop, at least for the moment.

"How does that still have power?" Justin asked as he hugged the front control panel.

"I don't know, but even if it loses power, I've got all the force I could get gripping the track. So long as the hydraulics hold out, we're okay. Besides, the last place we want to go is forward."

"What if the track doesn't hold out?" Stacy asked.

"I can't fix that." Darin shook his head.

"Can we walk back down the track?" Catherine asked.

"It will be tricky, but I think it's our only choice," Matt answered.

"Not with all that stuff falling out there, we'll be killed," Stacy whined.

"We can't stay here, Stace," Darin said.

"Is that really going to hold?" Matt tipped his chin at the robot arm.

"I think the pincer itself has an independent battery. It can keep us here, but that's it," Darin explained.

"So we need to get out and climb up onto the track and balance-walk our way back," Matt said.

"Or pull a Cody and swim our way to safety," Justin offered.

"I don't want to do that again," Cody said. "Rocks and dirt were hitting me. I almost got my clock cleaned by a boulder as big as my head."

"Neither choice is great," Darin growled.

The track shook and pitched them forward toward the reservoir. But the tram cars remained hooked together. Everyone braced themselves to stay upright.

One by one, each securing cable or metal support that

hooked the track into the ceiling popped like corks out of champagne bottles.

The vat line had done the same thing under stress, and Matt knew how that had ended. "We can't go back. There isn't time," he said.

The track leaned more deeply toward the reservoir, while the track behind them slanted up to where it was still attached to the ceiling. It might have seemed like a roller coaster if it wasn't so deadly.

"We're stopped," Darin assured them. "The robotic arm is holding our position. We've got to figure out the best way down."

"Maybe we slide down my rope to the water?" Matt suggested. "Better than jumping for it from this height."

"Can you shut up about your rope for a minute!" Stacy huffed, then buried her face in Darin's chest. "It's no use!"

"How about the causeway?" Cody suggested. "I'm done swimming."

"I know it looks bad, but it can't get any worse," Darin said.

The support points holding the track pinged and broke. The entire tram line pitched, and everyone was thrown forward as the tram hung straight up and down. Catherine and Justin slammed against the windshield. Stacy's back pressed against the front seats. Cody and Matt were thrown forward, leaning against the front doorway of the middle passenger car. Darin hung above them, holding onto the robot arm.

CHAPTER 31

Somehow, with the strength of the robot arm and the grooves of the tram itself, they were still attached to the track.

"You were saying?" Justin coughed.

"Are we dead?" Stacy squeaked.

"No." Darin's voice came out a little strained as he clung to the robot arm. "Like I said, it's holding. For now."

"Can we move?" Catherine turned her head to look out the windshield she was pressed up against.

"We're going to have to at some point," Matt said.

Darin nodded, frowning.

"Is everyone okay? That was quite the tumble," Cody said.

Justin and Catherine moved with care, lowering themselves closer to the front of the tram car, backs against the front wall. Stacy remained pressed up against the back of the front row of seats.

"It looks like it's attached firmly to the track, and

thanks to Darin's quick work with the arm, I think we're stuck here good," Matt said.

"Like a tick on a hound," Cody added.

"Why aren't you scared?" Stacy peered around the seat to look at the Texan.

Cody smirked. "Maybe cuz I already thought I was a goner twice today. I'm feeling numb to this roller coaster ride. Heck, I like 'em."

"Not me," she responded.

"I don't either," Catherine agreed. "If we ever get out of this, I'll never go on another one."

Darin released his grip on the robotic arm and landed spryly on the back end of the passenger car. Matt and Cody were ten feet below him and the others another ten feet beyond that. There was little they could use to climb up to his position.

"Everybody, take some deep breaths; we're going to have to get out of here one way or another, and soon," Darin said. "We'll need that rope again, champ. If there's one thing I'm glad about, it's that we decided to bring it along."

Matt nodded at him. "Thanks."

Catherine twisted around and glanced straight down the almost vertical track line. The swirling waters below moved, almost hypnotic, with the currents caused by the falling debris.

"Oh no." She gulped.

"I told you not to look down," Justin said.

"No, you did not!" she shot back.

"We're so high up." Stacy shivered and shut her eyes.

Matt withdrew the rope and looked through the windows for the walkway. It was much too far away.

"What are we gonna do?" Stacy's voice quivered.

"We'll figure it out," Darin said.

"How?" she whined.

"Shut up." Justin ground his teeth.

"Don't talk to her like that," Darin snapped.

"Everybody, take it easy," Matt said firmly. "We aren't gonna sit here forever, are we?"

"Maybe," Justin muttered.

Matt ignored him. "We'll figure it out. Let's all think on it and throw out some ideas. No wrong answers while you're brainstorming."

Darin looked back at the robotic arm. "If I release the arm's grip, we'll slide down into the reservoir. We'll all get down together, and then we can swim for that canal and spillway we saw."

"We'll be killed. Genius idea, *champ*," Justin spat.

Darin glared at him.

"Hey!" Matt snapped. "I said we were just brainstorming. Take it easy, we're all just trying to figure things out. This situation is too dire for us to start fighting amongst ourselves."

"*Dire?*" Justin mouthed mockingly. Catherine hit him in the shoulder.

Matt did his best to ignore the combative attitude. "I was wondering if we could toss my rope to the walkway."

"It's way too far," Darin said.

"What about with the robotic arm?" Matt looked up at him.

Darin shook his head. "It doesn't have that kind of kinetic force. It can lift great, but—"

"And spin," Stacy interrupted.

"And spin a rope, but it can't throw with any skill," Darin finished, nodding his head appreciatively at Stacy.

"I was thinking if it could spin things fast enough, we could wind it up and then have it throw a line with a weight attached," Matt suggested.

Darin nodded. "If we had the time, we could try and experiment, and maybe we could send a weighted line like you're saying, sure, but—and this is the big 'but' right now—as soon as the arm releases the track, we are falling down to the reservoir. We can't use the arm to throw anything."

"Then what are we gonna do?" Stacy asked with a dramatic shrug.

"Looks like all we can do is go down to the water and swim for it," Justin said.

"I don't have gloves anymore. I don't want to slide down the rope and burn my hands up and then try and swim," Catherine said.

"I could try and ease it down, then at least we're not plunged into the water," Darin said.

"Like easing your toes into a cold pool?" Matt asked.

"Well, more like jumping into the kiddie pool before you go into the deep end," Darin admitted.

"Ewww, kids, like, pee in the kiddie pool." Stacy winced.

"There's worse than that down there already," Cody reminded her.

Matt took charge again. "Let's have everyone buckle

up as best they can and try your idea. Maybe let's attach a rope to you since you can't buckle at all while you're manipulating the arm."

Darin shook his head. "I don't know what will happen, but I'd rather not get hung up on a rope if we go down fast. I'd rather take my chances jumping clear than being tied to the tram when it hits water. We don't know how deep it is, do we, Cody?"

"No idea," he answered. "I sure never touched bottom, not even when I fell a hundred feet. I must have gone under at least twenty feet, too."

"Guys, this is too dangerous," Catherine argued.

"We're out of choices, Catherine. We've got to try something before the roof right above our heads comes down on us. We have a ticking time bomb right now," Matt said as a handful of dirt fell amongst them.

"Okay," she said softly.

"Everyone, buckle up," Matt ordered.

Darin climbed back up the robotic arm, so he sat astride the base and control panel. "Everybody ready?"

"We're ready," Matt answered.

"We're ready! *Gajong*!" Justin waved his arms as if he were playing a guitar, mimicking the beginning of a Van Halen song.

Darin wiped sweat from his forehead and gingerly put his hands on the control toggle that both opened and moved the claw. He pressed lightly, and nothing happened.

He took a deep breath and repeated the motion.

"Everything good back there?" Matt asked.

The claw sprung open, and they raced down the track.

"Oh crap!!!" Darin hung on for all he was worth, desperately trying to get the claw to grasp the track again, but now they were falling straight down, and the claw could not get a grip. Instead, sparks and metal from the track flew behind them like a comet's tail.

Someone screamed.

The tram slammed to a stop, and Darin faceplanted into the control panel.

"You did it! Are you all right?" Matt asked.

"Am I bleeding?" Darin mumbled, staring down at his wet shoes. His hands shook from the force of holding the toggle and panel's switches during the plummet.

"No, we're in the water—and we're horizontal again! We might have to start swimming, though." Matt splashed at the water with his feet.

"Oh, Lance-Darin, you're a hero!" Stacy squealed. She slogged over to him and threw her arms around his neck.

"Good," Darin whoofed.

"It's a boat now." Stacy smiled.

They all looked about. They were upright and floating on the reservoir, while behind them, more pieces of the roof dropped into the water, causing waves and swirling eddies, which made them bob across the deep-green waters like a cork.

"Are we sinking?" Darin asked.

Cody shook his head. "Not yet, anyway. It's almost like it was designed to float like a raft."

"Now, if we just had a way to move this tub," Justin said.

"We'll find a way. We always do," Catherine said with a big smile of relief on her face.

"That's right," Matt agreed.

"Smooth sailing from here on out, eh, chief?" Justin slapped Matt on the back.

"I hope so," he answered.

CHAPTER 32

A long piece of tin crashed into the roof of the tram pod connected to the flatcar where they stood, admiring their luck at floating over the waves. They all dashed for the enclosed pod.

As Cody ran for cover, a splash of earth-covered tree roots doused the floating pod, blinding him. Stumbling back, he tripped on the sidewall of the flatcar. "Matt!" he yelled as he fell overboard.

Somehow, over the din, Matt heard him and raced headlong through the showering dirt and debris to extend a hand to Cody.

"We've got to get out from under this!" Darin shouted as he glanced about for a way to paddle the pod-turned-raft. "Stacy, grab that broom!"

They rushed back outside the pod to help Matt and Cody.

A girder splashed down not far behind them, sending a wave that pushed them away from the most dangerous of the falling debris.

Matt grasped Cody's hand, braced himself against the edge of the pod's plastic wall, and pulled him to safety.

Mud ran down the side of Cody's face, mingling with the blood from a cut to his jaw.

Matt gripped Cody's shoulders. "You all right?"

"Let's just say I don't feel like taking another bath just yet. But this ain't my first rodeo. I'll be okay." He grinned.

"Let's try and move this heap," Justin scowled, "before the rest of the roof lands on top of us!"

Without a means to paddle beyond the broom Stacy found, they reached their hands in and stroked in unison.

"This isn't working!" Stacy cried.

"Maybe we can use the robotic arm . . . if it still works?" Justin suggested.

"It's dead." Darin looked back at it. "Coming down that roller coaster almost tore it out of its housing."

Matt glanced about and pointed at the spillway. "If we can get to that canal's edge, we can climb down the spillway."

"To where then, Einstein?" Justin complained.

"Well, we can't stay here. Besides, it looks like the only way out of here," Matt said.

"He's right," Darin confirmed. "The rest of this is just a service basin. People weren't meant to be down here."

"If we're gonna move this, we have to work together," Catherine shouted over the chaos. "Half of us stroke together on this side and the other half on the other side. Hopefully, that will give us some kind of uniform force to move this thing."

They paddled as in sync as they could manage toward

the man-made spillway and the empty canal. It was slow going, since the pod floated but was not designed to be a streamlined boat at all. As they neared the edge of the concrete bank, Matt cursed under his breath. The sides were much steeper than they'd looked from afar.

"If I jumped out to that, I think I'd tumble right back into the boat," Cody said.

"Maybe with good climbing shoes, I could Spi-der-Man up that," Justin answered.

"Yeah, but you're not wearing good climbing shoes, are you?" Catherine glared at the concrete wall.

"Nope."

As they paddled, more debris fell from above. A heavy piece of metal, big as an engine, splashed water over the top of them, sending another chaotic wave that turned the pod about in the dizzying lake.

"Guys! Faster! It's gonna get bad," Darin shouted as he paddled furiously.

A big fan blade whirled down, slowly spinning as the last of its inertia failed.

Stacy screamed.

"Paddle! Everyone together!" Matt ordered.

They grunted and gulped in air as they paddled in unison in the other direction, but the sloshing reservoir waters made them spin almost in place.

Narrowly missing them, a careening fan blade landed like a giant's sword stroke on the edge of the reservoir, cutting into the concrete. Cracks formed where the blade hit, and water flowed over and through the damaged spillway, slowly at first, until the cracked barrier could no longer hold the water pressure back. Chunks of broken concrete flushed away in an instant, and the gouge grew larger as they watched.

"Look at that force. This must be a lot bigger reservoir than we can see," Darin said.

"Guys, I think we should get away from that," Catherine yelled, just before it ripped open like a deafening zipper.

Powerless to do much else, they all held on as the tram car raft was yanked toward the gaping wound in the reservoir.

"Paddle harder! All together!" Matt shouted.

They dipped their arms into the cold, dark water and stroked for all they were worth, but were pulled inexorably toward the open fissure. The gap widened as more pieces of concrete fell with the force of the water. Chunks battered and slid down the newly formed canal.

"This must be like how the Grand Canyon was formed," Justin said.

"Not now," Cody muttered, shaking his head.

The cascade of water swept them toward the spillway. The tram car slammed against the edge, held there for now, as it was still too wide to fit sidelong through the breach.

"Should we jump?" Catherine asked.

"It's too steep. Stacy couldn't make it!" Darin answered.

"Save yourselves," Stacy cried. "I'll love you forever, Lance-Darin!"

"I'm not leaving you. We have nowhere to run to yet, and this whole spillway is breaking up."

"You're breaking up with me?" Stacy gasped.

"What? No!" Darin shouted.

"Don't yell at me!" She broke into tears.

More cracks beside the spillway caused a full-on flood out into the canal, toward the open pipes on an opposite wall.

Matt turned to Darin. "We're stuck. Can the arm push us off or anything?"

Darin shook his head with a scowl. "I told you the arm is broken!"

"Can you just try it?" Matt asked, a note of desperation in his voice.

Darin rolled his eyes but took the controls and tried to move the arm. Sparks flew from the lower base, but the arm swung in spasmodic jerks and grabbed the side of the spillway. "It worked!"

The pincer of the arm held onto a piece of concrete connected to a protruding section of rebar.

"Now what?" Justin asked.

The concrete crumbled, and the tram cars whipped forward and slipped off the edge. They slid down at a forty-five-degree angle into a canal. They zoomed along, screaming as dirty water gushed over the top of the tram car, soaking them. The tram shuddered as debris slammed into the front of it and scraped underneath it.

"Hold on! It's gonna get worse!" Matt cried.

"What is it?" Catherine shouted.

"Duck low and hold on!" Darin dropped to the floor, abandoning his station at the arm.

A fan blade stretched across the canal. The tram cars slammed into the waiting blade, and the roof peeled back with a screech. Glass, plastic, and metal fragments covered the group.

A rending groan and thump sounded behind them.

"What was that?" Stacy asked.

"The arm!" Darin answered.

"What?"

"It's gone!"

The water, carrying them with it, rushed toward massive tubes sucking the water up. "That has to be where water goes to feed the floods or something," Matt said.

"Then we don't want to go there!" Darin grimaced.

"What should we do?" Catherine asked.

"I've got an idea," Matt said. "This canal is about as wide as the tram cars. Maybe if we all go to the back, hold on, and jump up and down, it'll drag us sideways and wedge us."

"Or it might just flip us over." Justin eyed the approaching tubes.

"Would we be any worse off?" Matt asked.

"No. Let's try it," Justin agreed.

They all crowded to the back of the flatcar. The bottom scraped against the concrete beneath with the added weight.

"Now, let's jump in place," Matt said.

They jumped, and as they landed in unison, the pod slammed against the bottom of the canal, forcing the car to catch on the bottom edge. The front-end car whipped about and wedged against the other side of the canal. The water hitting it sideways tilted the tram, nearly flipping it over into the turbulent water.

"That was risky," Justin said.

"Quick! Everyone out!" Matt ordered.

They scrambled out onto a concrete bank. Darin went last. He crouched to leap, and the tram car flipped, throwing him into the murky water.

"Lance-Darin!" Stacy screamed.

He spun end-over-end in the brown water. He righted himself and, with desperate strokes, tried to swim against the strong current to no avail. The unforgiving deluge carried him toward the big, open pipes.

Matt rushed forward, working to make a lasso with his rope, inwardly cursing himself for his dangerous plan to get them to shore, potentially costing his friend his life, and wishing he could be as good with a lasso as he guessed Cody was. But there was no time. His hands shook as he formed a loop in the rope and glanced up at the massive open pipes that gulped down thousands of gallons of water every second.

Matt tossed the looped end to Darin, who was spitting out mouthfuls of dirty brown water. Darin caught the rope, and it stretched taut as he vanished beneath the churning waters into the gaping black hole.

CHAPTER 33

"Lance-Darin!" Stacy cried. "No!"

"As long as he holds on, we've got him!" Catherine tried to comfort Stacy, who was awash in tears once more.

"Chill, it's going to be fine." Justin grabbed onto the rope behind Matt.

Catherine narrowed her eyes at Justin but said nothing as she rubbed Stacy's shoulders.

Matt, Cody, and Justin pulled the rope hand-over-hand against the flow of the water. Darin broke the surface with a sputter—alive and conscious, but coughing, gasping for breath, and almost drowned. As they pulled him onto the edge of the concrete bank, Stacy struggled to reach him.

"Hold on, give him some room to breathe." Catherine held her back.

Darin coughed up a gut-full of water.

"You all right?" Matt asked.

Darin nodded and coughed up another mouthful

before finally answering. "That was a ride I never want to go on again. The pipes look like they flow on this level, but they don't. That was a sheer drop down. Never would have gotten back if you guys hadn't pulled me up."

"Oh, Lance-Darin, don't scare me like that!" Stacy broke away from Catherine and threw her arms around his neck.

Darin struggled to draw a breath, but he didn't bother to make Stacy let go. His face flushed a little with the moment.

"Let me get just a little more of a breather, huh?" he finally said.

Stacy stepped back to give him space, but she beamed.

As Darin lay on the edge of the concrete bank, Matt glanced around at their new surroundings. There hadn't been much of a chance while they'd been riding the floating tram or fishing Darin out of the pipe.

Matt's eyes widened, and he pointed at two green steel doors, one on each side of the canal.

Darin's gaze followed the trajectory of his pointing fingers. "Maybe I was wrong, and people were meant to be down here to check on things."

"Two doors." Stacy looked back and forth between them. "Which one should we take?"

"The only one we can without swimming," Darin answered. "Besides, they probably connect together on the other side of the wall anyway."

"So the maintenance people could have gone everywhere down here," Catherine agreed.

"If maintenance people had been around doing their jobs, this thing wouldn't be falling apart," Justin seethed.

"I mean, how long have we been frozen for all of this to be in this condition?"

"Decades," Darin answered somberly.

There was a hint of gloom that hung over them at the thought. Matt gave himself a mental shake. "Let's go bust open that door and keep moving."

Justin raced ahead and kicked the door to no effect. Cody ran and tried the same maneuver, but the door held up to his assault too.

"Let me." Darin threw his full shoulder against the door. It didn't even budge.

Stacy raised an eyebrow at the boys, put her hand on the knob, and turned it. The door swung open on creaking hinges.

"I can't believe we didn't try that in the first place." Cody laughed.

"I just thought it would be locked." Justin shrugged. "Who knew it would be so easy?"

"I totally did." Stacy gestured at herself with a thumb.

A rare moment of laughter broke the tension.

"Come on, guys, let's check it out." Matt led them through the doorway.

Pipes of varying sizes covered the walls inside. Running water echoed through the massive plumbing system, and leaking water dripped from a few of the more rusted pipes. One spit a pin-sized leak at them like a squirt gun. The wall stretched the entire height of the subfloor. Dim lights shone at a wide doorway far ahead. Matt led them toward that light. They passed by ladders and scaffolding showing where workmen could climb up to check gauges and other apparatus among the multitude of pipes. Streams of water pooled on the ground and ran into musty-smelling grates.

Once they had walked the length of a basketball court, they passed through the brighter doorway into another walled-off section. The doorway was thick, and the passage extended almost twenty feet through a solid rock wall. None of the water pipes came to this side. This section housed an open bay with towers and different construction vehicles on different lift systems. It reminded Matt of a toy shop for a giant, with full-sized toy trucks on the shelves, just waiting for a gargantuan child to come and take them down.

The veritable lattice of vehicles reached close to the top of the subfloor, back up by the walkway.

"I can't hear the water anymore," Catherine said.

"I think all of that damage is behind us," Justin answered.

"Good riddance," Stacy said.

Matt nodded, looking up. "I think it's because we're on the other side of a big rock wall dividing the collapsing reservoir side from this garage. This area had to be built strong to hold all these vehicles."

"Stronger than holding a lake-sized reservoir?" Justin teased.

"You know what I mean."

Catherine broke in. "Guys, at least the building isn't coming down on us at this point."

"Should I be scared that I don't, like, think we're going to die right this second?" Stacy piped up. "I mean, is it a bad sign that nothing is happening to us right now?"

Darin held her close. "It's all right. There doesn't have to be something horrible every moment."

Matt looked at the trucks and elevators. "I think we're as far down as anyone is supposed to be."

"The basement?" Cody asked.

"Looks like, since this is the lowest the elevators go."

"So we can only go up from here," Catherine said with a smile.

"Exactly." Matt smiled back at her. "The walkway is way up there, but as long as these lifts are working, we can get up there and keep moving."

"Maybe we can even get one of these trucks working, and we can drive our way out of here," Justin said.

"Hot dog, that's a good idea!" Cody slapped his hands together. "Let's see what we can get running!"

CHAPTER 34

"Well, let's check them out!" Darin raced forward to look over a Humvee.

Stacy followed, giddy at the idea. "I've never ridden in one of these before."

"We gotta see if we can get it started first." He smiled down at her.

Several of the vehicles on the ground floor had their hoods open, as if someone had been working on them and then just walked away, never to return.

Catherine tried the door of a small pickup. "This one is locked."

"Break the window!" Justin said.

"I'm not gonna break and enter." She put a hand on her hip.

"Like anyone here will care," he responded.

Cody looked under the hood of the first truck he came to. "This one is missing a battery."

"So is this one," Matt announced. "It's almost like

somebody took them and hurried away. Why would they do that?"

"Maybe they were expecting an EMP and wanted to have extras in the shelter," Matt suggested.

"Like, what's an EMP?" Stacy asked.

"An electromagnetic pulse—it happens with nukes and maybe space stuff, like a flare from the sun. There was something I read about once called the Carrington Event. It happened back in like 1859. It fried all the telegraph wires."

"What?" Justin gasped. "No way, man."

"Really," Matt insisted, in all seriousness. "For all we know, that could be part of what this apocalypse is caused by."

Catherine had not broken into the locked truck, but moved on to another and announced, "There's no battery in this one, either."

"Let's keep trying," Matt shouted. "I don't think they could have taken all of them."

"Don't be so sure, chief," Justin said. "Every single one I've checked is missing a battery."

"As long as we can get even a hint of a spark, we can get them running," Darin responded.

"Don't even need the keys. I can hot-wire any of these." Justin laughed.

"Dang it!" Cody said.

"What?" Matt looked at his friend.

"I keep forgetting the time we've lost," Cody responded.

"So?"

Cody scratched at the back of his neck. "The gas has evaporated, and where would we drive to anyway?"

"B-35," Darin said soberly.

"It's been so dang long that any gas left in these has probably long since gone bad. The tram only worked cuz it was electric," Cody continued.

"We've gotta try," Matt said. "Doesn't diesel last longer?"

"Maybe. But without batteries, we're never gonna get any of these started and drive them anywhere."

"Plan B, then," Matt said.

"Which is what?" Justin asked with more than a hint of disdain.

"We climb up the tower of shelved vehicles as high as we can go. Back to a regular walkway, hopefully without any pitfalls and roofs falling in, and we keep going to B-35. We've got to do it with or without a ride."

Justin slammed the hood down on the truck he was looking at. "You're right, chief. If we can't drive, we might as well start walking."

"Climbing." Catherine pointed at the ladder and scaffolding.

"Ugh, why can't the elevators work?"

"The way things have been going, they'd probably drop us," Stacy said.

"I've still got the blueprints, and the walkway that leads to the mountain is right up over there." Matt lifted his chin to indicate the walkway.

"You sure about that, chief?" Justin asked.

Matt studied the blueprints he'd laid out on the hood

of a truck. "There's another tram up there. I say we stay on mission, find the mountain—and our parents."

"Do you think that's a good idea?" Stacy asked. "The tram, I mean?"

"If the roof isn't falling in, and we keep Justin away from the robotic arm, it will be fine," Darin answered.

"Hey!" Justin muttered.

"I'm kidding."

Matt folded the blueprints and shoved them back in his backpack. "Let's head up here." He led them past other abandoned vehicles, dump trucks, backhoes, and dozers. Reaching the ladder, they slowly ascended. Climbing was tiring but pretty efficient. There were landings on every story, and they could rest, even though their destination was almost forty stories up.

Halfway up, Stacy looked down the ladder and gasped.

Darin was right behind her and put a hand on her calf. "Don't look down. I'm right behind you, and we can do this, no sweat."

"I'm already sweating like it's the Fourth of July. Wait, does anyone know what day it is?"

"It doesn't matter anymore." Darin chuckled.

"Don't laugh at me," she snapped.

"I'm not laughing *at* you. I'm laughing *near* you. It was just funny to think about how days don't matter anymore, just right now."

"That makes sense," Stacy said as she continued her ascent up the ladder.

"This reminds me of climbing the radio tower on the top of U Hill back where I grew up," Justin said.

They reached the top row of vehicles and looked over toward the walkway. "I thought you said this would connect?" Justin complained.

The long climb had not brought them to the walkway. Instead, they were parallel to it, separated by almost twenty feet. Twenty feet that stretched out over the gap, including a drop of more than two hundred feet. There was a collective sigh. Matt had promised them a simple walk, and now they were faced with a crevasse.

"Hang on, guys, I think we can get over there," he said.

"How?" Stacy cocked her head to the side and tapped her toes on her good foot, as if he had just told her they would have to walk home from the mall.

"I've got my rope," he said cheerily.

"You and your damn rope," Justin scoffed.

"It saved my life." Darin narrowed his eyes at him.

"Yeah, but—" Justin stammered.

"Yeah, but what? Hear the man out," Darin insisted.

"Thanks." Matt lifted his chin toward Darin. "Anyway, if I can find something to use as a grappling hook, I think I could shimmy over. We all could."

"Not me," Stacy said. "I might as well start climbing back down now. Come on, Darin."

"No, he's onto something. Besides, we don't know what way down there would get us back to the walkway. I didn't see any other stairs or anything."

"This is the only way," Matt said, glancing around the back of a suspended truck that was parked on the side of the vehicular elevator. "This will work," he proclaimed, holding up a vehicle jack.

"Don't tell me. This one has a battery?" Justin asked, still teasing the concept.

Cody shook his head. "Gas would still be bad, even if there was one."

Justin frowned.

Matt ignored the discussion. He really wanted this to work. He hated the idea of making everyone climb all the way back down just to hunt for another route to the walkway and farther on to the mountain, where their parents lay in frozen slumber. This had to work.

He tied the end of the rope to the heavy jack, hoping it would function like a grappling hook. He threw the jack like a shot-put over the railing, hoping it would snag and wrap around the walkway. A loud clang echoed throughout the massive garage when the jack connected with the metal. But it did not hook around the railing like he'd hoped, and it pulled loose. He pulled the rope to him, preparing to try again. Justin sighed loudly, and Stacy rolled her eyes so aggressively, Matt swore he *heard* it.

It took a few attempts before he got the jack to snag on the railing and the support structure. He tugged on it hard to be sure it held tight. He tied his end to the frame of the shelving. It was almost even and straight across. Matt laughed to himself. *Finished my Eagle Scout badge forty-something years ago. Guess it really stuck with me.*

"Looks good, boss," Darin said.

Matt pulled on the rope one more time to test its hold. "Here she goes," he muttered. He grasped it with both hands, then kicked his legs up over the rope. He hung there for a moment as they all waited, holding their breath.

"You okay?" Catherine asked.

"Yeah, just making sure that if it went slack and dropped, I'd still be right next to you guys," he said.

"Well, next time, give us a warning, huh?"

"Sure," Matt said.

The rope bowed a little bit, and the metal railing made a slight creak, but the jack held true. Matt pulled himself, hand-over-hand.

He was about halfway when the jack slipped a little, and the rope dropped a couple of inches.

Catherine gasped.

"It's okay. It's holding fine," Matt assured her. He looked down. He dangled over the open-air bay of vehicles. The drop was greater than when he had come down the air shaft, but then it had been dark. Now everything was all lit up, and he could see the gray concrete floor as plain as day. It disturbed him more than the dark had. He lost focus, and his legs slipped off the rope. He dangled by just his hands.

"Matt!" Cody yelled.

"I'm fine. I wasn't paying attention." Matt grunted as he readjusted his grip.

"Focus, man," Darin boomed.

Catherine held her hand to her mouth and looked away.

"Idiot," Justin muttered.

Matt breathed heavily. This was a little more difficult than he thought. It had been a hard day, and they were all pushing themselves to extremes. It took a few attempts, but he got his legs over the rope again.

"Don't scare us like that," Cody shouted.

"Sorry," Matt answered. The coarse rope burned the back of his calves. But he kept going until his hand finally touched the cold metal of the railing. He made it. Matt breathed a sigh of relief and awkwardly climbed onto the walkway.

"You did it. Good job," Darin shouted.

"Thanks!" Matt made sure the end of the rope with the jack handle was secure and tight. "All right, you saw me do it. We can all do it and keep going."

Stacy folded her arms. "I can't do that. You're stronger than I am, and you almost fell!"

Matt shook his head. "Stacy! I quit paying attention for a second and let myself slip. It was dumb, but I'm okay, and guess what? We've been doing these amazing things on our journey to find our parents all day. You have done awesome things all day, and you can do this too! I know you can. I believe in you. Darin believes in you. We all do!"

"You really think so?" she asked.

"I know so. You climbed down the elevator shaft. You got out of the fertilizer vat. You helped us in the freezer. You can do anything you set your mind to."

"You promise?"

"I absolutely do!" His stomach twisted a little. *I hope.* Doubt crept in. *What if we lose someone else because of one of my ideas?*

"Okay, I'll try," she said.

Darin helped her get on the rope and looped a short safety line to her to give her a little more confidence. She went hand-over-hand and slid her ankles along the line until Matt could reach her and help her down to the walkway.

"See? I told you, you were amazing." The tightness in his chest eased just a bit.

"I don't remember you saying that." She blushed.

"Well, you are," Matt said.

CHAPTER 35

Darin was last and looped the rope about through the railing on the other side and attached it to himself as a safety line, so once he got to the other side, they could unravel the loops and keep the useful line. This was one tool that was too valuable to leave behind.

"Everyone good?" Matt asked after they had all rested from their climb for a few minutes.

"I'm great! Amazing even!" Stacy beamed.

"I think we're good to go," Catherine said.

"All right." Matt wiped sweat from his forehead. "The blueprints say we should go this way, and we should be close to another section where we can find a tram and get to the mountain."

They joked together as they walked; all of their moods improved. The causeway curved in an easy arc several blocks long and took them away from the reservoir and solid rock wall that helped retain it.

Justin, walking in front with Catherine, suddenly stopped. "No way."

"What?" Catherine asked.

"Look at that!" He pointed.

A hundred yards in front of them stood an elevator.

"What's the problem?" Darin asked.

"Another elevator. Where the tram was supposed to be. Chief here isn't interpreting the blueprints right," Justin accused.

"There's a long platform. For sure the tram would have stopped here," Matt countered.

Darin glanced over the prints. "Maybe because it's a long ride up?"

"Guys," Catherine interrupted. "Let's not fight. Let's just see if it works and keep moving." She pushed the button. Motors groaned on the other side of the doors. From behind the steel doors came the telltale whine of cables operating.

"It's moving," Cody mused, "but why isn't the door opening?"

After a couple of minutes, Stacy suggested, "Maybe it's broken."

"Then let's find another way," Catherine said. "Let's look at the blueprints again."

Darin studied them. "There's another junction back the other way past the wall we walked through earlier, so we could go check that out."

"Isn't that where the roof fell in?" Justin said.

"Maybe not as far as we floated and walked," Catherine said. "When the tram finally went down, we could see far on the opposite wall that the track was still there, along with other doors and things."

"Well, if the door isn't opening, we better go another

way." Matt's shoulders slumped a little. He felt a lot of pressure to be the voice of reason and try to keep everyone's spirits up, but leading them to false starts was not the way to do that. He rolled up the blueprints, thankful they didn't get so wet as to ruin them, and put them safely in the backpack.

Just as they began to walk away from the elevator, the doors moved apart with a screech of metal-on-metal and a pressured *whoosh*.

"I'm so tired of hearing metal grind," Catherine said. "What's happening now?"

They all turned in unison. The elevator doors were partly open, beckoning them to enter.

Cody rushed forward to keep them from closing.

One of the doors stuck halfway, so Justin pushed it open the rest of the way.

"Is it safe, though?" Stacy asked. "I mean, why did it take so long to open?"

"Maybe it had a long way to go to get here; the blueprints did make it look as long as a tram track," Matt guessed.

Darin looked inside. "I think it's old, but I don't see any water damage."

"What about the parts you can't see?" Justin asked.

Cody scanned everything he could as well. "Old, but looks solid and clean."

"Let's go, then," Catherine said.

"We've got to keep moving," Matt agreed. They all crowded inside.

"Look at that. It's almost like a window." Stacy

observed a clear plexiglass side that revealed a concrete wall beyond.

The doors slowly closed, and the elevator jerked and started to rise.

"Did someone hit a button?" Catherine asked.

"I didn't see one," Darin said. "Must only go between two floors?"

The elevator rose, and through the plexiglass, they watched as they moved beyond the ceiling of the subfloor. They saw a floor grate with several feet of dirt above it.

Stacy cupped her hands around her eyes and pressed them up against the scratched, foggy window to try and see more of the world outside while the elevator rose. "This is like the Steamtown Mall, where you can look down on the food court four levels down," she said. "But where is the top?"

Almost in answer, they passed by massive metal beams and I-beam roof trusses, then multiple cables and pipes hidden inside a dark outer housing.

"This is the mountain," Matt said as he pointed at the blueprints. "We're almost there!"

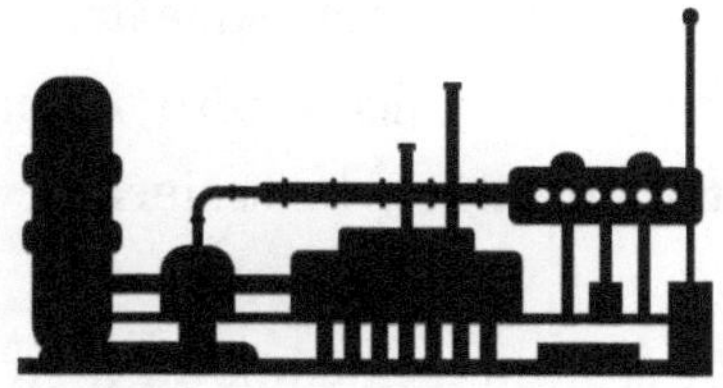

CHAPTER 36

The elevator bumped along slowly.

Matt grinned and grabbed Catherine's arm. "We're getting close!"

"You really think this might be B-35?" she asked.

"Yes." Matt let his hand linger on her arm, enjoying the flush of warmth it brought him.

"Everything is so fake," Justin complained. "Why here?"

Matt shrugged. "It's all man-made. This could be an extension of HZRD. This could be the cavern. We've traveled a long way from where we were topside, past the trucks, and where Nathan . . ."

"I know what you mean," Catherine interrupted, taking his hand.

Justin slowly nodded. "Sorry, chief. I sure hope you're right."

The elevator continued rising, and the tension and excitement of where it might stop had all of them glancing about anxiously.

"Can't wait to see my folks again," Cody said with an *aw shucks* grin.

"We're almost there," Stacy squealed, taking Darin's hand. "I'm going to introduce you to my parents!"

Darin was the only one who seemed devoid of excitement.

The elevator slowed and came to a stop. The doors crept open onto a large room.

Matt raced out ahead of everyone, shouting, "Mom, Dad, I'm here!" He ran halfway across the room, then slowed and looked back at the others.

"What is this?" Stacy asked.

"Looks like a control room," Darin said.

There were panels with dials and pressure gauges. Red, yellow, and green buttons blinked off and on in different sequences.

Matt raced about, searching in every direction, but it was apparent there was no cave, and that this was not where anyone was cryogenically frozen.

The room had windows all the way around, granting a view of the valley beyond. A multitude of computer screens and empty chairs revealed that at one time, a lot of people had worked there. But everything was covered with a thick film of dust.

"I wanted to believe you were right, Matt, but this is worse than not knowing where they are!" Catherine shouted. "Giving me hope and then taking it away is breaking me!" She covered her face, awash in tears.

Some of the computers were broken. Cracked and broken switches sparked occasionally. Old lab coats hung on the backs of swivel chairs and hooks on the wall and had the logo for Demo Trench sewn onto the left breast pocket. Two parallel lines with a sphere in the lower third. A single slanted line on the right side of the double lines. Underneath the logo were the letters "HZRD."

Matt slid his thumb over the frayed threads of the logo patch. "What is going on here?"

No one answered.

Levers labeled for each of the disasters resided on a panel in front of one of the windows. The room was painted a sickly light yellow. Clocks, tickers, gauges, and dials were embedded in machines labeled: "Blizzard," "Flood," "Heat Wave," "Tornado," and on and on.

Matt had rushed to the hallway across the room, opening and closing the doors all along the walls, only glimpsing inside the rooms long enough to see there were no cryopods within. At each room, he yelled frantically, "Mom? Dad?"

"They're not here!" Darin shouted. "And even if they were, they couldn't hear you!"

"Mom! Dad!" Matt raced to the next room down the hallway.

Stacy tugged on Darin's arm. "Somebody has to stop him. He's losing it."

"Dude! Stop! Take a breather!" Darin shouted. "This isn't the vault!"

Matt came back to the main room and stopped. Tears streaked down his face. He glowered at the machines. "They made all this just to torture us!" He kicked the nearest one until the exterior paneling fell off and the mechanical guts were revealed. He tore at colored wires, then picked up a chair and slammed the legs into the machine. Sparks showered the floor. The panel snapped and popped. Matt covered his eyes with his arm.

"Please, stop before you hurt yourself or one of us!" Catherine cried.

Matt looked at her, his chest heaving in anger. He threw the chair and dropped to his knees.

"They were supposed to be here!" Matt cried. "Argh!" He screamed and seized another chair and threw it against a window. The glass splintered into an ugly, spiderweb-like pattern but didn't break all the way through.

"Matt! Please, stop. We're here for you!" Stacy cried. "You're, like, amazing too!" She rushed toward him, and the others followed.

Stacy and Catherine wrapped their arms around him as he fought to hold back the tears.

"They were supposed to be here," he murmured.

"They're still out there somewhere. We just got to keep looking." Darin put a hand on Matt's shoulder.

After a few silent moments, Cody said, "Let's take stock of what's in here and go from there."

"You're right." Matt looked his now oldest friend in the eye. "Thanks, Cody. Thanks, everyone. I'm sorry."

"It's okay. I'm sorry too." Catherine hugged him tighter. "It's hard for all of us."

Darin sighed. "I agree with Cody. Let's see what we can find out in here. There's a lot to look over. There's a big bookshelf, and maybe we can log into one of these computers and read some files or something."

The bookshelf sagged under the weight of dozens of drab-green three-ring binders labeled with things like: "The Mission of Site HZRD," "Motion Sensor Diagram," "Demo Trench Emergency Operations," "Ecological Simulations," "Manual Overrides," and "Environmental Maintenance."

"Maybe these can tell us more about what's out there." Matt pulled down the manual that had "Emergency Operations" written on the spine.

Darin, Matt, and Cody looked through the manuals while Justin, Stacy, and Catherine stared out the windows.

"We're really high up here," Catherine said. "No wonder the elevator took so long. It's like you can see our whole world from here."

Stacy shouted with glee as she looked out the window, "Guys, I think I can see Camp New Beginnings! Over there!" She tapped her finger repeatedly against the glass until everyone came to look. In the distance, they recognized the camp.

"Over there is the junkyard," Matt said.

"Look at all the holes in the ground! We came through that!" Cody said.

"Under that, you mean," Justin corrected.

"I think this is telling me how to turn it all off." Matt thumbed through the manual.

"It can't be that simple," Darin argued.

Matt gave him a grin and strode over to a control panel. "It says that there's a lever that has to be pulled back once, pushed forward, then back again to cause an emergency shutdown of systems. I think it's this one." He laid a finger on a big lever marked with "DO NOT TOUCH" and "Emergency Shutdown."

"How do we know that won't make things worse?" Justin asked.

"What could be worse than what we've already gone through?" Matt asked in return.

"Good point, chief, give it a whirl!"

Matt followed the instructions, pulling the lever back from its middle position, then forward, then back once more. He had to put quite a bit of muscle into it, using both arms. It sure didn't feel like it had ever been done before.

The sound of gears that had been just vague white noise before suddenly became apparent as they ground down to a halt, and the general mechanical hum went silent. The mountain shuddered once and went still.

Stacy gasped. "Please tell me we aren't dealing with earthquakes up here."

"I think it's just part of it all shutting down," Darin assured her.

"Wait a minute," Matt said as he skimmed through the manuals.

"What is it?" Darin asked.

"More tricks," he lamented.

"What do you mean?"

"This." Matt pointed to a spot in one of the manuals denoting the mountain.

"What?" Darin asked again. "I don't know what you're saying."

"How high do you think we are on this mountain?"

"I don't know, looks really high up. I'm not great with distances, but I'd say a half mile or so?"

"I was guessing something like that."

"Okay, so?" Darin asked.

"Well, it's more tricks. They've built this place with forced perspective, and here is the proof. It says the mountain is only two thousand feet tall," Matt explained.

Darin squinted at him. "I don't follow."

"Amusement parks do this all the time, like Disney's Matterhorn. They all use this forced perspective. It's all part of the trick of how this place is made up. Now I just need to find something that tells us how big this park, or whatever it is, is!"

"I think I understand you now," Darin said. "There must be some kind of limit to how big an area they can control, but it is pretty big."

"Guys, what is that?!" Stacy called out.

"What?" Matt asked.

"Something is falling from the sky. Out there in the forest."

CHAPTER 37

"That was weird," Justin said. "What the heck could that have been?"

"I don't know," Matt answered, "but I know where we can get some answers."

"Don't tell me. The Bible," Justin said with more than a hint of sarcasm.

"Manuals actually." Matt handed him one that was labeled "Motion Sensor Diagrams."

"Thanks," Justin muttered, reluctantly taking the manual and flipping it open in the middle. Darin and Cody started looking through other manuals.

"I'm hungry. We're going to look in these other rooms for some food or something to drink," Stacy said.

"Be careful," Darin called.

"We will," Catherine said.

"Listen to this." Matt read aloud. "'This mountain command structure is HZRD. It's not A-67 or B-35. The mission of this area of this building is to evaluate and train personnel to survive an artificial apocalypse in anticipation of a real event.'"

Justin guffawed. "I'd call bull crap, except for everything we've already been through. This is totally unbelievable. There is no way my parents knew we were getting signed up for this garbage."

"I think you're right," Matt said. "But listen, there's more weird stuff. Remember when they tried to slow the apocalypse by detonating a bomb in the Mariana Trench? It didn't work, obviously. It says here that the world government built multiple buildings like HZRD. There are three within the vicinity. The idea was to train families to eventually survive the apocalypse, since it wasn't just going away. The think tanks figured that if they could train people with all the skills they needed to survive super-bad, man-made disasters, then they could survive the real apocalypse."

"That's messed up," Justin said. "Everything we've been going through was a training mission?"

"No, it wasn't," Darin snapped. "We weren't supposed to do anything like that. Westbrook is the mad scientist that dumped us in this hellhole."

Matt interrupted them to continue reading. "This says that, at first, they brought in soldiers and other specialists to survive inside HZRD and learn to adapt through all possible outcomes. Soldiers came in, it worked okay, most survived, but some died. There're notes about those that died."

"That's awful. How could they think this was a good idea?" Cody asked.

"Power corrupts. Some egghead in a lab coat talks

and holds a clipboard, and then everyone else just goes along with it because they think they can trust the expert," Darin said bitterly. "Follow the leader if he has 'authority.'" He held up his fingers for air quotes.

"Nailed it." Justin nodded.

"I've got the handwritten logbook here," Cody said. "The last page says that this HZRD site was abandoned. The operation was to be forgotten, and they wanted to move to the second phase, plan B, which was to get everyone into cryosleep and into the cryovault. That's what was recommended by the team of scientists running this. It was called the 'Save the Population' project."

"Crazy," Justin said.

"They all lied," Darin snarled.

"Our parents didn't lie," Matt said. "They just believed what everyone was telling them: 'For the good of the world.' I think so many people were working on this, some had good intentions."

"Good intentions will get us killed," Darin snapped. "Men like Westbrook built this place, and it's all a big lie designed to kill people just to satisfy their—"

"Easy," Matt said. "Take a breather if you need to. We're all friends here, just trying to figure it out."

Darin nodded, snapped his book shut, and sat on the floor with his back against the wall.

Matt read on. "'Power to the vault and HZRD complex is all geothermal, from natural volcanoes on account of the bomb messing the land up.'"

"Molten energy," Cody said. "Interesting."

Matt shrugged. "Weird; I figured everything must be solar-powered here, but I guess not."

Justin broke in. "Okay, it's my turn. I've got the manual on motion sensors. There's a big diagram showing all the motion sensors. They're everywhere, to keep an eye on where people are and then make things happen! Some even look like tree branches just so you can't see them. But that's what triggers all the crazy weather."

"This is messed up," Darin said from where he squatted.

"What did you find, Cody?" Matt asked.

"I found a lot on how to fix and maintain all the inner workings of the machines and stuff," Cody answered.

"Last thing we want to do is fix any of that crap!" Justin said.

Stacy and Catherine came back with a handful of dried food and a few cans. "I even found some warm soda." Catherine held up a can. "Did you guys find anything out?"

"We did. We got an idea on where we are and what this is all for," Matt said.

"We've got to figure out where to go now and what to do," Justin said.

"Is there anywhere safe?" Stacy asked.

Justin pushed the manual away from him. "The Sev was safe, and it had no motion sensors."

"Motion sensors?"

"Yeah, they're everywhere, waiting for us to trigger the crazy weather."

"Which is all turned off now, we hope." Darin took a granola bar from Stacy's outstretched hand.

"Maybe going back to the Sev to live is the best plan?" Catherine said.

"I don't want to stay here. I want to go find my parents." Matt studied the book in his hands without really seeing it.

"You know that's not what I meant." Catherine touched his arm. "Just . . . we need to get some good rest and be safe and then go on to wherever it is we have to go. I don't know if you've taken the time to think about it, but we've had a very rough last twenty-four hours and really need some good sleep before we keep pushing ourselves so hard, or we're all gonna drop."

"Was it that long?" Stacy asked.

"I have no idea how long we were in the subfloor," Catherine said. "I was guessing."

Matt looked at her. "You're right, we have been pushing ourselves really hard, and we need to be safe when we rest. Maybe the Sev is our best bet."

"We had one heck of a party there." Justin chuckled.

Cody nodded toward a window. "It's getting dark now. Maybe it's been two days."

"You ever gone two days without sleep before?" Darin asked.

"I ain't never had two days like this before," Cody said.

"You guys have been reading all these books to figure this stuff out?" Stacy asked.

"Yeah?" Matt raised an eyebrow in her direction.

She held up one of the manuals. "Well, this one explains the sun."

"What?" Darin exclaimed. "The sun?"

"Yeah, it's always cloudy but has never looked right. It says here that there are just a bunch of lights hung up high everywhere that are on a timer. It's nighttime, so it's dimming down like at my friend Wanda's house. They had lights on a dimmer switch in the living room."

"No way." Darin stood and looked over her shoulder at the manual.

"This says the timer is right over there." Stacy pointed at one of the control panels. A red digital clock read "dusk." "Like, let's see what happens if I turn the knob."

"This will be good," Justin said.

Before anyone could tell her to stop, Stacy twisted a big red knob, and as the readout turned back to "afternoon" in digital letters, the lights outside brightened as if she had turned the sun back up to full.

"I'm the queen of summer!" She laughed.

"This place is a madhouse." Darin groaned as he gave himself a facepalm.

Catherine unwrapped a dehydrated fruit package. "This place doesn't seem to be the most comfortable. There's food and stuff, but it doesn't feel as homey as the Sev did."

"What else did you two find?" Matt asked.

Stacy's eye widened. "There's a room with lots of guns!"

"Guns?" Cody asked.

"Yeah, and bio-hazard suits and gas masks," Stacy added.

"There's a kitchen or cafeteria with food. Mostly cans is all that's left—the Sev had a better variety." Catherine shrugged. "There's a mechanics shop that smells like oil, but it has tools, and then there are sleeping quarters, and the last thing we found at the very end of the hall is another elevator."

"Why didn't you tell us about that?" Justin snapped.

"I thought you would rather eat first," Catherine replied sharply.

"Well, you're right," he said, half apologetically.

Matt popped open a soda can. "Let's stay the night here and resupply. We can figure out where to go in the morning."

"I could make it morning now, if you want." Stacy gestured, queen-like, to the digital clock.

"No!" came the collective response.

"Jeez, guys, like, take a joke from your queen of summer," Stacy said, kicking her toe at the floor.

"I want to go back to the Sev," Catherine said.

"It's late, and you said we need rest," Justin reminded her.

"Yeah, but I don't feel safe here. At least there I could relax."

"I want to get out of here entirely. If it's just a big complex with halogen lights for a sun and fake weather, I want out, period." Darin scowled, looking out the windows.

"Maybe we should vote on it," Cody suggested.

"What do you think, chief?" Justin asked.

Matt hadn't been expecting that. He was wrapped up in all the terrible revelations of the last hour. He had been wrong about so much. This mountain was not where their parents were. He had risked all of their lives for what? To play with a fake sun?

"Guys," he said, his voice cracking just a little, "I

don't want to sway you in either direction. I've been wrong, and we didn't find our parents. We almost got killed multiple times. I've failed you all. Someone else should take charge of the situation."

"We'll vote on it," Darin said. "Everyone write down your vote, and we'll tally it all in the morning after we've slept."

"So vote for Matt to keep being the leader and get us out of here?" Stacy whispered a little too loudly.

Darin shook his head. "Elevator or Sev, Matt stays the leader."

CHAPTER 38

They went to sleep in the barracks area of the control center. And while there were no windows and they slept as late and long as they felt like, there wasn't a general feeling of rest once they all awoke and got up for a breakfast of canned dry oatmeal and peaches.

Catherine handed Matt a can containing everyone's votes from the night before. "Here you go."

"Thanks, Catherine, but I don't need to be the one to decide anything."

"You're not. We voted, and we didn't vote about you leading us." She shrugged. "Honestly, you and Darin have been awesome down here, but you're the one who found this place. You got us here. It's unanimous. You're the head counselor."

Matt paused for a moment. Counselor. Arriving at Camp New Beginnings felt like a lifetime ago. So much had changed in just a few short days. "Unanimous? Even Justin?"

"He looks up to you more than you know. He's just prickly sometimes."

"All right, I'll count the votes now, everyone," he said louder to all those gathered about the table.

Darin and Stacy stood close by. "This is anonymous, right?" she asked.

"It is if you didn't sign it," Darin said.

"Yeah, but wait. Matt, can you, like, recognize our handwriting?"

"Not yet," he answered.

"Okay then, the queen of summer says you may proceed."

Darin laughed at Stacy's antics and gave her a peck on the cheek.

Matt counted the votes. "First one says: 'Go down the elevator.' Second one says: 'Go to the Sev.' Third: 'Elevator.' Fourth: 'R&D.'"

"R&D?" Justin asked.

"It's the Sev," Stacy explained.

"Oh yeah." Justin shrugged

Matt continued. "Fifth: 'Elevator.' Last one: 'Elevator.' So it's two to four, elevator, and I guess that means continuing our search for our parents instead of waiting it out at the Sev."

Catherine hugged herself and slumped against the back of the chair. Matt knew she'd voted to go back to R&D, but wasn't sure who else had voted that way—maybe Justin?

"Well, regardless of where we all wanted to go, we need to get gear and backpacks," Darin said. "And anything else that will come in handy for the apocalypse."

"Guns?" Stacy asked.

"Sure," Darin said. "Even if I don't know how to shoot, I figure one of you all do, right?"

"I've shot guns." Catherine folded her arms. "Though I don't know how shooting at the rain will help."

"Loads of times." Cody nodded. "Gophers on the ranch will break a horse's leg."

"Once," Matt said sheepishly.

"I never have, but I want to," Stacy said.

Justin stayed silent, revealing well enough that he had never shot a gun either.

They grabbed green army-style backpacks and filled them with dried foods from the cafeteria, as well as any other useful supplies they could find.

Cody found full-face oxygen masks and oxygen tanks in the biohazard area. "These are like what firemen use."

"You think we might need those?" Stacy's eyebrows scrunched together.

"It's a crazy world out there," Cody answered.

"True." She nodded, her red hair bouncing.

Matt reminded them as they loaded blankets and food into the packs, "Leave any cans that even hint at bulging. That means they're bad, as in poisonous."

"We know, chief."

Fully stocked up and ready, they rounded the corner and pushed the button to the elevator.

CHAPTER 39

The elevator buzzed like a microwave, as if it were powering up. The doors swiftly opened, functioning much better than the other elevator.

"Sounds like we should have ridden this one up in the first place," Justin said.

"Well, I didn't see it when we got in the other one," Catherine said.

They crowded into the elevator. With their stuffed backpacks, extra oxygen tanks, tools, and guns, the small space was rather squished. It was quite a bit different than when they had come up.

"Are there any buttons?" Matt asked.

"I don't see any," Darin said. "But the other one didn't have any either. Single destination lines, I guess."

"Maybe we should take the one we know, since we don't really know where this one goes." Catherine bit her bottom lip.

But it was too late. The doors slid closed, and to their

surprise, the elevator shot off sideways, slamming them into the side and each other.

"How is it doing this?" Justin pushed off the metal wall and regained his balance.

"I don't know. I've never heard of anything like it. Darin?" Matt asked.

Darin shook his head, steadying himself with a hand pressed against a waist-high handrail.

"It must be on a track like a tram instead of cable—but why not just have a tram?" Cody questioned.

"I knew we shouldn't have got on this thing." Catherine dropped to her knees. "Make it go back."

"It's all right, Catherine. It's running smoothly." Matt crouched and gently rubbed her back. "I don't think we're in any danger of it falling apart or anything. It's a much smoother ride than yesterday's elevator."

Matt picked at a hangnail and felt a small bubble of panic creeping into his thoughts. He stared at the back of Catherine's shoulder, the burned skin peeking out the top of her shirt. Focused on the rippled skin, he counted slowly to ten and back. His Matt-itation. He felt his breathing and heart rate return to normal. He couldn't wait to tell his mom how helpful it'd been. Tell her in person.

"How much longer? This feels like it's been–"

"It's been ten minutes," Darin said. "I found a watch." He held up his left wrist, a black-banded watch encircling it.

"I thought you said it didn't matter, like, what day it is. Just *right now* matters, silly," Stacy reminded him.

"Yeah, but when I found a watch, I wanted it. Just

had to wind it, and it worked. Now I can keep track of how long it takes us between destinations."

"Elevator rides should not be this long." Catherine wrapped her arms around her abdomen. "I'm getting sick."

"Probably those canned peaches," Justin said.

"More like the oatmeal, ack." Stacy poked a finger into her mouth. "I mean, gag me with a spoon."

"Stacy, please," Catherine choked.

"Sorry."

The sideways elevator traveled for over an hour. They couldn't see out, and pressing any of the irregular buttons inside the service panel did nothing to slow its humming speed.

"Maybe we're not even moving, and we're still right beside the hallway, but this thing is broken and just vibrating to make us think we're going sideways, because we all know elevators totally don't do that." Stacy's eyes widened.

"It sure feels like it's moving sideways to me," Cody said.

"It's doing more than just vibrating." Darin placed his palm on the wall.

Stacy shrugged.

"I am tired of this!" Catherine shouted.

"It is weird," Darin said. "Maybe we should try and open the door."

Matt looked to Cody. "You've got a crowbar, right?"

"Yep." Cody took his pack off and reached for the tool. They tried to get it between the doors, but to no avail. The seal was too tight.

"What about the ceiling? I've seen people in movies escape elevators by climbing out the ceiling," Justin said.

"It's worth a shot." Matt shrugged.

They pried at the ceiling panels but only succeeded in taking off a decorative tile, revealing a solid steel roof to the elevator.

"Well, that's that. We're trapped," Cody lamented.

"Can we tear apart the control panel?" Justin asked.

"We might end up trapped inside in the middle of a long tunnel," Darin said. "Whoever made this meant for people to get whisked around long distances. I think we need to just wait it out. Everyone get comfortable. Who knows how much longer this will be."

"How long has it been?" Stacy asked.

"One hour and twenty-seven minutes."

Catherine cried into her sleeve.

"Well, let's get comfy," Matt said.

He spread his gear out over the floor, and everyone followed suit, trying to make themselves comfortable. Cody turned his pack into a chair, but Matt couldn't get his to sit right.

"What if it just keeps going forever?" Stacy asked.

Darin hushed her as Catherine started to cry softly again. Matt put an arm around her and pulled her against him.

The elevator slowed, then dropped for a couple of seconds before coming to a dead stop.

"It's done?" Stacy looked wildly back and forth from Matt to Darin.

"Let's hope." Matt removed his arm from around Catherine and rubbed his hand over his buzzcut.

"Be ready for anything," Cody said as he cocked his
gun.

Matt gripped his own gun but wasn't ready to cock it.

CHAPTER 40

They waited for what seemed an eternity, but it was just a few seconds until the doors slid open to yet another small control room, only ten feet wide by thirty feet long. The walls were padded, off-white, and cracked with age.

"What is this place?" Justin asked. "A looney bin?"

"I have no idea," Matt answered.

"There's a window back there." Cody slowly moved forward, his gun at the ready.

As they entered the room, the elevator door closed behind them with another *swish*, and then an airlock door closed, and the loud hissing sound of forced air echoed in the room.

"It's a trap! Get the masks on!" Matt ordered.

They struggled to get the masks and air tanks on— several were not connected, and Stacy panicked as she tried to get hers to snap closed over her face and hair. Darin assisted her and then stroked her hair to calm her, since their voices were muffled by the masks.

"Is there poison gas in the room?" Catherine asked.

"Don't know, let's look around," Cody said.

The room remained as it had been when the elevator opened.

Cody signaled them forward toward the window. Only Matt joined him.

He reached the circular window and peeked out. General fogginess greeted their view upon a bleak landscape. A meteor way off in the distance plummeted to Earth and sent black soil flying into the sky. Matt's heart raced. Actual snow fell in the fog, and an even stronger blizzard raged off to their left, while dark gray ash fell to the right. Hot and cold. Barren landscape . . . red and scorched.

Matt shook his head. "We're in the middle of a frying pan that's in the deep freeze."

Cody went back to the air ducts and examined them and the outer door that was sealed shut. He took his gas mask off.

"You sure that's smart?" Justin asked.

Cody nodded. "I think this was just ventin' because we came out of the elevator, and it was adjusting for the pressure differentiation. Probably need the masks again if we open that door that goes outside, though. I'm guessin' that's why all that apparatus turned on in the first place."

"Well, what's outside, then?" Catherine asked.

"Take a look," Cody offered.

"Out of the fire and into the freezer that's on fire," Justin said.

"What do we do?" Stacy asked.

Darin shook his head.

"We should have just gone back to the Sev," Catherine said.

"You want to get back in that elevator?" Justin taunted.

"I didn't say that," she snapped. "I said we never should have got on that *hellevator*!"

"Nice," he snapped back.

"Guys, take it easy," Matt said. "It's important that we know everything we can about where we are and what's out there as we try to find our parents. Darin, is this like what you said you had to drive through to get to Camp New Beginnings?"

Darin shook his head. "It was bad, but this is really different."

"Well, we either need to go on or just go back to the Sev and sit on our hands. But I think we need to keep going and get out of this place."

Catherine put her hands on her hips. "Tell me I'm wrong all you want, but I've always stood by you, Matt Voorhees, and I'm telling you I want to survive. And if that means making the best of what we do know is safe—R&D—then I think that's what we should do!"

"I'm not saying you're wrong for wanting to be safe, Catherine, but we can't sit back and keep eating old food. If we're gonna get out of here and rescue our parents, we need to keep moving."

"We could go back to the control room," Justin offered. "At least we know that's just an hour-and-half ride away."

"The Sev *was* pretty dang comfy," Cody said.

Stacy raised her hand. "R&D."

"We don't even know if we can survive out there." Catherine folded her arms like she had won the debate.

"You're right," Matt said. "We don't know. But I've got to find out. Hang on a minute, okay?"

Darin nodded.

Matt put on a gas mask and waited for the others to do the same before he opened the exterior doors. Again, the air venting system kicked on and blasted all of them inside with fresh air as Matt stepped outside.

The ground was black and caked with ash. Far behind the new control room and doors where his friends crowded against the glass to watch him, he could see the false mountain. His feet dragged in a tar-like substance near a wavy yellow line. Asphalt and potholes led to another mountain in the far east. The road had been severely damaged by volcanic action, or maybe from the falling asteroids—the real adversary of the Earth. The real apocalypse.

Matt hurried back inside, allowing the vents to do their work before he lifted his gas mask up. "I'm going to find my parents or die trying. Who's in?"

To be concluded . . .

As a kid, Tyler H. Jolley always had a knack for storytelling. When he grew bored of old fables, he created his own exciting and unique worlds. Many years later, he still had so many new ideas and stories swirling in his head, but with nowhere to share it. That's when he put his pencil to paper and let the creative juices flow.

His debut novel, *Extracted*, came out in 2013 and swiftly became an Amazon Best Seller and Spencer Hill Press Best Seller. *Prodigal* and *Riven*, the second and third books in The Lost Imperials series were released in May of 2015.

After a brief hiatus he restructured and returned to writing. His Adventurous Ali series has received much praise. To date, he's released three in the series.

When he's not writing, you can find him at his orthodontic practice, mountain biking, or on the hunt for the perfect doughnut.